"Robin . . . get out of here," Michael ordered **huskily.**

She shook her head slowly, and deliberately stepped closer, her hands lifting to rest on his broad chest. The dark, damp hair covering his muscled flesh was a tactile delight, and her fingers stroked it compulsively. She hadn't realized he would be so beautiful, and the sight of him moved her more than she would have believed possible. "I can't do that," she murmured.

"Robin—"

She rose on tiptoe, her arms sliding around his neck, her body molding itself to his. And she could feel his instant response. His eyes were darkening, and a muscle leapt in his jaw. As if he couldn't help himself, his arms wrapped around her body.

"Damn you," he whispered, just before his lips covered hers.

Robin felt the instant surge of heat, the wildfire running through her veins. He pulled her even more firmly against him, and a sound she didn't recognize tangled in the back of her throat.

He was taking her, possessing her, demanding with a force she'd never encountered before meeting him. But something in her answered that force, in a battle, a clash of wills, but she didn't know what they were fighting.

Or fighting for. . . .

WHAT ARE *LOVESWEPT* ROMANCES?

They are stories of true romance and touching emotion. We believe those two very important ingredients are constants in our highly sensual and very believable stories in the *LOVESWEPT* line. Our goal is to give you, the reader, stories of consistently high quality that may sometimes make you laugh, sometimes make you cry, but are always fresh and creative and contain many delightful surprises within their pages.

Most romance fans read an enormous number of books. Those they truly love, they keep. Others may be traded with friends and soon forgotten. We hope that each *LOVESWEPT* romance will be a treasure—a "keeper." We will always try to publish

LOVE STORIES YOU'LL NEVER FORGET
BY AUTHORS YOU'LL ALWAYS REMEMBER

The Editors

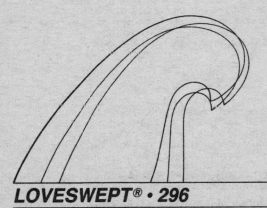

LOVESWEPT® • 296

Kay Hooper
Captain's Paradise

BANTAM BOOKS
TORONTO • NEW YORK • LONDON • SYDNEY • AUCKLAND

CAPTAIN'S PARADISE

A Bantam Book / December 1988

Published simultaneously in the United States and Canada

Bantam Books are published by Bantam Books, a division
of Bantam Doubleday Dell Publishing Group, Inc. Its trademark, consisting of the words "Bantam Books" and the
portrayal of a rooster, is Registered in U.S. Patent and
Trademark Office and in other countries. Marca Registrada.
Bantam Books, 666 Fifth Avenue, New York, New York 10103.

PRINTED IN THE UNITED STATES OF AMERICA

O   0 9 8 7 6 5 4 3 2 1

Prologue

Hagen was annoyed. He was always irritated by delays in the execution of his plans, and since this was a particularly vital plan, he was more than usually annoyed.

"Where?" he demanded, speaking flatly into the mouthpiece of his telephone, equipped with a scrambler.

"Just gone, and his men with him." The voice that replied to Hagen's question sounded hollow because of the scrambler, yet not even the technological device to prevent interception of telephone conversations could leach from it all indications of a strong and dynamic personality.

"You can't even tell me where?" Hagen asked.

A rueful sigh came over the wire, and the voice replied with an underlying layer of mockery that made Hagen grit his teeth. "No, I can't. I've been tracking that bunch for months, as you very well know, but this time they've given me the slip. Sue me. Now, if you want the women—"

"No," Hagen said, allowing himself to grimace since he was alone in his office. "That's the quickest way of committing suicide I know." He muttered the comment, but his voice was clear and distinct nonetheless.

"That's was my reading of the situation. In any case, the bait for your trap is momentarily out of reach. I'll keep looking if you like, but I have to tell you the chances are slim until he decides to surface again. I wouldn't be surprised to find out he'd gone to ground."

"What?" For the first time, Hagen was honestly shaken. "Impossible!"

"Chief, every soul in that whole bunch has terrific instincts. You may think your little tests these last months have been subtle, but what you left out of the plan was a culprit."

"There was no need to—"

"No?" the voice interrupted sardonically. "You think they aren't going to get suspicious when some unnamed enemy tests their security more than once? If I were in the place of any one of them, I'd be very busily trying to find out what the hell was going on. You'd better take it as a yes—that's what they're doing."

Hagen was silent for a moment, then offered what he knew was a weak objection. "They wouldn't leave the women unprotected."

"Unprotected? Remember what Kipling said about the female of the species, Chief? Take that as a yes too. Those ladies need protecting about as much as a battleship does. You want my advice, you'd better back off for a while."

Hagen ignored the advice. "Where's the yacht?"

"*Corsair?* No sign of her in her usual area. They may be aboard her, but she could be in the South China Sea for all I know."

"Have you checked with Captain Siran? He may—"

"Sorry, Chief. He's unavailable."

Hagen's voice began to lose its forced patience. "Why is he *unavailable?*"

"Took a leave of absence for personal reasons."

"What aren't you telling me?"

There was a brief silence, and then the voice said, "Just that you can't count on Siran at the moment, Chief. He has his own fish to fry."

Hagen heard more than the words. Bluntly he asked, "Daniel, what's going on?"

The sigh this time wasn't wry or mocking; it was weary. "What goes around comes around. The captain has his hands full with a specter out of his past."

"He's alone?"

"He didn't even give me a chance to argue with him."

After a moment Hagen said, "If anyone can handle himself, it's Siran. I could have used his help, however."

"Yes. Well, your plans are on hold for the time being."

"You're absolutely sure you can't locate them?"

"Afraid I can't. You wouldn't think a public figure of his prominence could disappear so quickly or so thoroughly, but he does seem to have the knack of it. So you have two choices, Chief. Either wait until he shows himself—however long that takes—or try to find out where he is from one of the ladies. The former being preferable to the latter, if you ask me."

Hagen swore softly. "Agreed. If I show any interest at all, Raven will be onto it instantly."

"You train your agents too well," Daniel noted dryly.

"That wouldn't bother me so much," Hagen retorted irritably. "if only they'd *remain* my agents." He sighed. "I don't suppose you'd be interested?"

Daniel chuckled softly. "No. You and I would no doubt lock horns. No, thank you; I'll stick to my own bailiwick."

Unsurprised, Hagen said, "It was worth a try. Well, keep me advised. And, if you hear from Siran, let me know."

"Yes."

The connection was broken.

One

When she was plucked, drenched and shivering, from the angry gray-green Atlantic, her first instinct, her only instinct, was to cling with all her remaining strength to the warm, wet arms that had saved her. And cling she did, like a desperate thing, until the man managed to break her grip and wrap her in a dry blanket.

A part of her consciousness was aware of being stripped of her wet clothing, swiftly and efficiently, of being dried briskly and dressed in something loose that was thick and warm. A cup was held to her lips and a fiery liquid flowed between her teeth, stopping their chattering. Then the softness of bedding was beneath her.

After that, only blackness, but it was blessedly warm and dry.

Her sluggish, weary mind surfaced a few times, vaguely aware of a faint light, of the lifting/falling motion of a boat on the sea. But nothing really registered, no single impression demanded that she think, and so she did not. She slept.

When she finally woke to the dim understanding that she was not where she should be but that where she was was better, the soft light still burned and the rocking motion had lessened. In an instant she identified the tiny cabin of a boat.

She was on a boat. But . . . she had escaped from the boat. Terror stirred in her sluggish mind, thick and suffocating. Or had it been a dream?

A dream. All a dream, of course, especially the bad parts. It was such a comforting notion that she accepted it instantly.

"Drink this."

It was a command, uttered in a hard masculine voice. Inured to commands delivered by hard masculine voices, she obeyed. Pushing herself into a sitting position, she accepted a cup from a sun-browned hand. Sipping, she identified coffee laced with brandy. It tasted good. Only then did she raise her eyes to look hesitantly at the man.

The rest of him was sun-browned too, she saw. And since he was wearing only swim trunks and an unfastened windbreaker, she could see a great deal of his muscled body. It looked as hard as his voice and obviously possessed the kind of raw strength that could never have been earned in a gym. He had almost-black hair and sharp eyes and was, she thought, the most handsome man she had ever seen.

Still, she had been too close to danger too recently not to recognize it in this man. It was apparent not only in his tight jaw and firmly held lips and in the strange, shuttered gleam of his gray eyes; danger was an almost visible aura surrounding him, enclosing him.

Detached, she transferred the thoughts to images, and saw steel forged in a white-hot crucible, still dangerous to the touch.

"What the hell," he asked in a quiet, rough voice, "were you doing floating in the ocean miles from shore?"

"Which shore?" she asked, feeling a flicker of interest.

He was sitting on the edge of her bunk leaning toward her. His eyebrows shot up at her question, then drew together in a frown. "Florida," he said brusquely.

"Oh." She considered the information, then answered his original question simply. "I don't know."

After a moment he said in a flat tone, "You're covered in bruises and have a few minor cuts. There are no signs of a head injury." He reached out suddenly, taking her right wrist and stripping back the sleeve of the heavy flannel shirt she was wearing. "Judging by these and your dilated pupils," he said harshly, "I'd say you decided to fly without wings and jumped off somebody's yacht."

She looked down at the bruised injection sites on her inner arm, and her mind fought to throw off the sluggishness. But it was difficult, and trying to concentrate made her head ache sickly. He thought she was someone's party girl, she realized, and had the dim recollection that she'd been wearing an evening gown when he had pulled her from the water.

"Did you see a yacht?" she asked, meeting his gaze.

"No." Almost absently he pulled the sleeve down

and smoothed the material before releasing her arm. "But, as I said, you were miles from shore. And right in the party crowd's playground."

"It might have been a yacht." She frowned at the cup in her hand, trying to think, trying to remember. "I believe it was a yacht. A big one."

His breath escaped shortly in an impatient sigh. "Was the party in full swing, or will someone have reported your disappearance?"

Her mind was clearing slowly. "No. No, I doubt there was any report."

He swore, the sound angry and abrupt. "Then I'll have to alert the Coast Guard. Is there anyone else—"

"You don't understand." She stared at him, wondering with a paranoia inspired by the last weeks if she could trust him. While he stared at her impatiently, she made up her mind. She needed a place to rest and gather her thoughts, to plan. It wasn't over yet; she couldn't let it be over. But she needed time. If she surfaced too soon—

"What don't I understand?" he demanded.

She took a long sip of the laced coffee. What a strange voice he had, she mused. Quiet yet hard. She drew a deep breath. "There wouldn't have been a report, but not because there was a party. There wasn't a party. They saw me go overboard. They . . . they shot at me. I was escaping," she ended in a rush.

"What?"

Seeing the disbelief in his face, she realized dismally how it all sounded. Melodramatic. Unreal. Like something between the covers of a novel or in cinematic Technicolor.

She looked down at her flannel-covered arm and

spoke softly, tonelessly. "They kept us drugged so we'd be quiet. But the drugs didn't work on me at first. That's why the bruises. I didn't know what was going on most of the time, but when I came to once, there seemed to be a storm. The others were still unconscious, but I thought I could get help if I could just get off the boat. Everyone was busy because of the storm. I managed to get topside and . . . and jumped. I heard a yell, and then guns, but the water was rough and it was raining. . . . With any luck, they think I drowned."

The man stared at her for a long moment, his gray eyes unreadable, something strangely taut in his expression. Then he stood, filling the small room, and took a step away from the bunk to reach for a bottle and glass on a nearby shelf. He splashed liquid into the glass and drank. Only then did he ask tersely, "White slavers?"

She was surprised at his quick comprehension, and wondered if he was just humoring her. But something about his hard face denied that possibility. When he turned to stare at her again, she nodded slowly.

"How many besides yourself?"

There was, she thought briefly, an element of unreality about the entire situation—conversation and all. This man was not reacting as she would have expected; he was neither disbelieving nor horrified. Nor did he seem sympathetic about what she had clearly been through. Instead, his tone was blunt and matter-of-fact, his expression remote.

"There were five of us," she said, trying to analyze his reaction, fit it into some niche in her mind. "All blondes and—and redheads." Her hand went briefly to her long, thick auburn hair.

"Did you know any of the other girls?"

The question confused her, which was hardly surprising, she thought, considering the befuddled state of her mind. "Know them?"

"Names," he said impatiently. "Ages, backgrounds. Did you know anything about the other girls?"

"No. Not when we were first taken aboard. We were strangers. We didn't have much of a chance to talk; they started the drugs right away. I know the other redhead's name was Marcy."

"What about the blondes?"

She looked at him, feeling a stab of uneasiness. There was something wrong with the question, and she didn't know what it was. She couldn't read his face. She wondered if anyone could. It was a closed face, giving away nothing. Slowly she said, "One was named Susan, I think. I'm not sure about the other two. They were—well, they looked like models. Mid-twenties, long fair hair, almost white. Sun-bleached, I guess."

"Both of them?"

"Yes." She stared at him, increasingly puzzled when she sensed more than saw this reaction to that. She could have sworn he was disappointed. Then he shrugged, as if to himself, a curiously wry twist to his lips.

"Any idea where you were bound?"

"I couldn't get the route; they didn't talk that freely in front of us. But from what they said, I gathered our destination was somewhere in the Middle East."

His expression had grown preoccupied, his gaze distant when he put the empty glass aside and sat on the edge of the bunk again. After an unblinking appraisal of her, he said dryly, "And just how did you manage to get yourself shanghaied?"

Not quite ready to be that trusting, she said, "I went to a nightclub. In Miami."

He appeared to accept her explanation. Slowly he said, "I suppose you'll want to notify the police—"

"No!" Realizing how sharp her response had been, she held her voice calm with an effort. "No, I don't want to report it. Those men . . . they play rough. If I went to the police, I'd be a loose end, a target. They think I'm dead. I want to leave it that way."

His eyes had sharpened, and now searched hers intently. "I see. You're probably right. What's your name?" he added, abrupt again.

It was, curiously, an out-of-sync question; normally it would have been one of the first asked. She wondered about this man's priorities. "I'm Robin Stuart."

"Well, Robin Stuart, my name's Michael Siran. I fished you out of the water about eight hours ago just off Key West. It's now six A.M. and we're approximately five miles off Key Largo, dead in the water."

"Heading?"

"Miami."

She nodded, trying to sort through her thoughts. "I wish I knew where . . ."

"Where the yacht went? It'll have to stick fairly close to land for a few days; if they planned a water route anywhere, they'll have to postpone the trip or make other arrangements." He sounded preoccupied again, as if something disturbed him.

"Why?"

He looked at her, gray eyes shuttered. "Because

the Coast Guard and various other law enforcement officials are patrolling very heavily. Rumor has it that an indecently valuable shipment of drugs is coming into the country via water. Everything that floats is being inspected bow to stern, and nobody leaves or enters U.S. territorial waters without due inspection unless they're very, very lucky." His expression was unreadable. "I was searched last night a couple of hours before I found you. I'd guess that the slavers are lying low for a while."

"But that's just a guess," she said steadily. "If it's really that—that hot, they may kill the girls. We were on that boat for at least two days before I got away. They can't hope to keep the others hidden indefinitely, and if they can't send them wherever they're supposed to go . . ."

For the first time, a flicker of what might have been sympathy showed on his hard face; her sudden guilt was obvious. "You couldn't have helped them," he said quietly.

Robin stared down at her empty cup and chewed her bottom lip. "They're just ordinary women," she said softly. "With ordinary lives. In Florida on vacation, most of them. No family, no one to worry or make trouble over their disappearance." She looked up at him suddenly, surprised by a fleeting look of pain on his face that was instantly gone, as though it had never been.

"There was nothing you could have done," he maintained flatly. "Your getting away was sheer luck. And since you never saw the yacht—"

"Maybe I did see it," she interrupted, staring at him, banking a great deal on that brief pain she'd seen. Or thought she had seen. "And maybe with a little help I could find it. Then I could tip the police, and they could search the boat."

After a moment he said levelly, "Around a thousand miles of coast in Florida alone, and you expect to find one yacht?"

She held his gaze determinedly. "One very large yacht. It's big, I know that. Manned by a large crew." She took a deep breath. "Judging by where you found me, it looks as though that boat sailed down along the keys. Their heading—would you guess South America?"

After a slight hesitation he nodded.

"But they can't get safely out of U.S. waters now. So they'll probably hole up somewhere near the Ten Thousand Islands south of Cape Romano."

"You know the coast." It was neither approval nor question, but simply a statement of fact.

Robin was still pursuing possibilities. "There's too much traffic near the keys; they wouldn't want that. And the southeast coast of Florida of congested. But they'd want to remain far enough south to run for it if necessary. It has to be the islands. If they still have the women, they have to be there."

Michael Siran shook his head. "It isn't a case of *have to be* anything. They could have slipped through the net, gotten away free and clear before they were spotted. Or they could be sailing calmly up the coast, where they'd find a plane somewhere to fly the women out."

"But there's a chance the yacht is lying low, waiting," she insisted softly. "Isn't there?"

He nodded reluctantly. "A slim chance. But no chance at all of finding it," he added.

"Help me," she said simply.

He ran a hand through his thick dark hair, staring at her impatiently. "Didn't you hear me? You haven't a chance in hell of finding that yacht! With or without me. It could be anywhere. It would take days to search the western coast, and it wouldn't be a thorough job even then. And looking for a boat in these waters! Even if you found one you suspected, you don't have the Coast Guard's authority to board and search."

"I'll recognize at least three of the crew," she said flatly, repressing a shudder. "I'll never forget them."

Michael stared at her for a moment, then said roughly, "Those bruises. Did they—"

"Rape me?" She shook her head. "No, not that. Apparently our *buyers* wanted their merchandise untouched." Her tone was bitter. "But they seemed to feel that a few bruises would heal before we were delivered. I fought the drugs, and them, so I was punished a few times."

"All the more reason—" he began.

Robin felt desperate. She couldn't leave the girls to the less than tender mercies of those slavers. She just couldn't. She hadn't meant this to become personal to her, but after sharing a terrified, drugged haze with young women who had no one else to care about them, the matter *had* become personal. Very personal. But she needed help in order to help them. And something told her that if she could only sway this man, his help would prove to be invaluable.

"Please," she said.

He was shaking his head, an impatient frown drawing his flying brows together. "No. Everybody in these waters is jumpy as hell right now, and it's no time to play detective. Look, I'm sorry. I'll take you back to Miami, and that's all I'll do."

She searched his face for a moment, looking for something she didn't find. No softening, no hesitation. He seemed almost angry, definitely brusque. He was also, she realized, worried about something, and he was tired. Very tired.

Robin looked down at the cup she was still holding. The coffee was cold. "They're so alone." She wasn't trying to convince him, just talking. "We all had that in common, being alone. And being afraid. And there was—" She stopped suddenly, remembering. "There was someone else, I think. At least one other girl. I heard her crying one night, in the next cabin. She sounded awfully young, like a kid . . ." Her voice trailed off, and she blinked back the hot pressure of tears. When she looked at Michael Siran, his face seemed to waver, to grow indistinct.

Robin blinked harder and felt her heart lurch oddly. He was looking at her, a sudden pallor obvious beneath his tanned face. His gray eyes were chips of steel, and his lips were pressed so tightly together they seemed carved of granite. She almost shrank away from him, conscious of an instinctive fear that was primitive, as if she had stepped into a cage where some savage beast crouched in wait.

It took only that instant for Robin to realize that he wasn't seeing her at all. It was something else he saw, something dreadful. But before she could begin even to guess what it was, the terrible expression was gone.

"All right," he said flatly.

•   •   •

Robin wasn't entirely sure she had done the right thing in asking Michael Siran for help. Something about the man bothered her, made her wary. He neither moved nor spoke quickly, yet there was something almost electric about him, like a force of nature imperfectly contained. And all her senses reacted to that force, even in her dazed state, just as they would have reacted to a storm. She was aware of him on some level deeper than thought, curiously made more aware of her own body, her own beating heart. She didn't trust the sensation.

She didn't really trust him.

Still, there wasn't much she could do alone, so there had been no choice. But she was disturbed by the entire situation. It would have been nerve-racking enough to try fighting her way through this mess alone; being unexpectedly partnered with a strange man who had had a sudden and inexplicable change of mind about helping her was even more unnerving. And he didn't offer to explain his change of mind. Immediately after agreeing to help her, he told her she could join him on deck if she felt up to it, and that she could find clothing to fit her in one of the built-in drawers beneath the bunk.

Left alone, Robin slid off the bunk and stretched sore muscles. She didn't know how long she'd been in the water the night before; it had been dark when she'd jumped overboard. The sleep had done her good, but she was still a bit tired and groggy.

In the bunk drawers, she found a pair of cutoff jeans that were close to her size—obviously not Michael Siran's—and a black T-shirt. The clothes fit her better than the baggy sweatpants and flannel shirt he'd dressed her in the night before, and she changed with relief. The evening gown she had worn had been ruined by the saltwater; she felt no regrets at losing it, but she wished now that she had been wearing a bra.

Still, she acknowledged wryly to herself, it hardly mattered. After all, Michael Siran had stripped her naked. The realization made her a bit self-conscious, and she pushed the feeling away only with effort.

She went slowly up on deck, finding herself on a relatively small cabin cruiser. The sun was still low in the east, and she saw no other ships near them. As far as she could tell, they still headed in the direction of Miami. The inboard motor started as she stood gazing around, and she made her way toward the small bridge. She paused only once, catching sight of an old-style life preserver hanging beside the cabin door. The name of the boat was stenciled on the white doughnut shape, and it made her pause in more ways than one.

Black Angel.

Great. That was just great. Robin wasn't overly suspicious of omens, but it struck her with a chill that she was involved in a dangerous situation, partnered with a stranger she hardly trusted, and aboard a boat named for the angel of death.

She blamed the chill on her still-groggy state, squared her shoulders, and went on to the bridge. He was at the wheel, gazing ahead with a slight frown. She took the opportunity to study him unobserved, unsettled to discover that she was abruptly aware of her heartbeat again. There was something compelling about this man, something that kept her gaze on him like iron filings to a magnet. Tall, lean, and hard, he reminded her again of a storm, caught in a moment of stillness, like lightning in a photograph. It was hard to breathe suddenly, and she fought off the sensation with determination.

"Are we going to Miami?" she asked.

He glanced at her, the brief look taking in her change of clothing without comment, then looked ahead again. "Yes."

"Why? The yacht wouldn't have sailed toward a congested port— "

"There's someone I have to get in touch with."

Robin waited, but he didn't elaborate. She stifled impatience, beginning to realize that this man wasn't going to be very communicative. "Who?"

For a moment it seemed he wouldn't answer, but then he said, "Someone who may be able to tell us something."

At least he had said "us," she thought. "You mean something about the yacht I was on?"

"Possibly."

Robin folded her arms beneath her breasts and leaned back against the doorjamb. "For instance?"

He glanced at her again, one eyebrow rising. "You sound annoyed," he noted dryly.

"I am annoyed. I'm not just along for the ride, you know."

After a moment he said, "You lost the first bout with these animals; sure you want to try for two out of three?"

Robin kept her voice even with an effort. "No, I don't want to do that. I want to beat them this time. I don't want them *in* jail, I want them *under* it. I asked for your help, I didn't ask you to do this alone. I can—"

"What can you do?" he interrupted. "Can you handle a gun?"

"If I had to, I'm sure I could."

"If you had to? Life or death, you mean?"

"Yes, I suppose that's what I mean."

"And when will you make up your mind about that?"

She frowned at him. "About what?"

"About when this becomes a life-or-death situation." He didn't wait for her to respond. "You were kidnapped, drugged, beaten, and shot at when you tried to escape. Now you intend to look for those same men and put them away for the duration of their natural lives. Needless to say, they won't accept that fate meekly. They may decide, given the chance, to shoot at you a bit more. Is that when you plan to shoot back?"

"If it comes to—"

He swore roughly. "Little fool."

Robin stiffened. Angrily she said, "You have no right to say such a thing! You don't know anything about me or my abilities."

He half turned to stare at her, keeping one hand on the wheel. "No, I don't know you," he agreed flatly. "But I know *them*. I know their kind. They don't give a sweet damn about the sanctity of life, Robin. They solve every problem with guns and violence, and they'll solve the problem you present the same way."

She almost flinched from the hardness of his voice—especially with the memory of too many other hard voices still rawly alive in her mind—but made herself remain still. Her chin lifted. "And I know *that*. I'm not a fool, whatever you think, and I'm not stupid. But whether you like it or not, I'm a part of this. For one thing, I know what that yacht looks like."

"Do you? One yacht looks pretty much like another."

"I can identify some of the men."

"If you get close enough."

Robin's frustration grew, and she tried to keep her voice calm and level. She felt cold inside, and afraid and alone, and the thought of facing those men again terrified her, but she couldn't let him see that. "Mr. Siran—"

"Michael," he interrupted, adding sardonically, "since we're in this together."

She ignored the tone. "Michael, you weren't with those girls. I was. I felt the needles, and the cruelty, and the terror of being kidnapped. I felt the horror and anguish of believing I'd be bought and used and sold like a piece of merchandise." Robin was hardly aware that her voice had gone flat and steely, but it didn't escape the man beside her.

She took a deep breath. "This is my fight a hell of a lot more than it is yours. I'll do anything I have to do to stop those men. Anything. That's something you can *count* on."

"I see."

Robin wondered if he believed her. She wondered if she believed herself. She was so afraid. And this time her fear could endanger others rather than just herself. This time her fear could get someone killed.

"Robin . . ." He hesitated. "I understand how you feel. You were degraded, even dehumanized, by what happened to you. And now you're mad, and you want to get even."

"I want justice."

"Be honest with yourself." He turned his head to give her a long, steady look. "You want to get even."

Reluctantly she admitted, "That's part of it. But not all. I want to help those other girls, and I want those men stopped."

Michael turned his gaze forward again. "All right. But this isn't a game for amateurs."

Her curiosity about this man had been growing, and she took advantage of the opening. "Which you aren't?"

He was silent for a moment, and then shrugged. "Which I'm not," he agreed flatly.

"You're an—expert at dangerous games?" When he remained silent, she probed determinedly. "You weren't surprised by white slavers; most people would be. You talk about men of violence as if you know them well. You sail a boat named for the angel of death. Tell me something, Michael. What do you do for a living?"

He smiled. "I run a charter service."

Robin silently weighed his tone, which was flippant, and studied the quick, somewhat menacing smile. Oddly enough, she wasn't afraid of him, but she thought a great many people would be. "Are you a smuggler?"

Michael didn't seem surprised by the question. "No."

"Gun runner?"

He shook his head slightly, and seemed amused. "I notice you've placed me squarely among the bad guys," he commented.

"Am I wrong in that?"

His look of amusement faded. "No. No, that's where I generally tend to be. Among the bad guys."

On impulse she said, "But you wear a white hat?"

He glanced at her, and his face hardened. "Dirty gray, maybe. White hats don't stay clean very long, Robin. Filth rubs off."

It was a disturbing comment, but because of her own background Robin was less unsettled than many would have been; she came from a long line of police officers, and knew what Michael meant. It *was* a dirty business, policing your own people, especially when the minority of those people, the lawbreakers, were often in the filthy business of using their own kind as a means for profit.

But it nonetheless bothered her that this man could well be the kind of man prevalent in her own family: the tough, fearless, confident kind of man who was a born police officer. In the last few years she had learned to resent some aspects of that kind of man, particularly the trait of fearlessness. They made it look so *easy*, those men, and at times she had hated them for it.

Because what came so easily to them was something Robin would have given anything to possess: courage.

She looked at his big, powerful hands on the wheel, and felt her throat tighten, her mouth go dry. *Damn . . . Oh, damn . . .* She dragged the traitorous thoughts back into hiding, refusing to give in to this mad attraction. Fiercely, she concentrated.

"Are you a cop?" she asked, almost hoping for a negative response.

Michael seemed to consider for a moment, then shrugged. "Something like that."

"DEA?" she asked, remembering his knowledge of the "rumored" shipment of drugs in these waters. If he was one of *those* men, she thought painfully, then he certainly had courage in spades. The people who worked in drug enforcement had the dirtiest, most dangerous jobs of all.

"I've done work for them from time to time. Miami has been known to be a center for drug trafficking, and this boat gives me a certain amount of mobility."

"Are you working for them now?"

"You're a very inquisitive lady."

Robin refused to be put off. "On a need-to-know basis, I think I need to know. Is that why you suddenly decided to help me find that yacht? Because those animals could be running drugs as well as being slavers?"

"I'm not working for anyone at the moment," he answered finally. He was gazing forward, frowning.

"But you aren't a captain."

"Of course I am. I even accept charters occasionally." His voice was dry again.

Robin's journalistic talents were at the forefront now, and she probed with careful concentration. "So it's just a cover?"

"What were you doing in Miami?" he parried.

"Vacation. Are you based here?"

"If anywhere. Where are you from?"

"San Francisco. And you?"

"The East."

"The Far East?" she asked gently.

He smiled a little. "No. East Coast."

Robin reflected that he was adept at not answering questions, but that only increased her curiosity. "About your work," she began determinedly, but was cut off.

"Miami is a long way to come for a vacation," he

said smoothly, "when you're from the West Coast. Why here?"

She gritted her teeth, but her voice remained calm. "You know what they say about summers in San Francisco; I wanted to bask in the heat down here."

"L.A. would have been closer."

"Smog," she dismissed promptly.

"There are other cities on the West Coast."

"I wanted to visit Miami," she said irritably, even more annoyed that she was losing her calm. "Look—"

"Robin." His voice was quiet, but it still possessed the peculiar trait she had noticed before, like something hard and dangerous covered with deceptive softness.

"Yes?" She felt oddly uncomfortable.

"If you want the truth from someone else, you'd better not offer lies yourself."

"I don't know what you're talking about."

"Don't you?" He half turned to face her, expressionless. "You aren't down here on vacation. You have some kind of background in police work, otherwise you wouldn't have asked the questions you did with such calm. Most people don't have the faintest idea what the DEA is. And if an average vacationing young woman got herself shanghaied, managed to escape, and was pulled from the ocean by a stranger, she wouldn't calmly ask him if he was a smuggler or a gun runner. And it isn't likely she'd decide to take on her kidnappers with or without his help. The most likely reaction to what you've gone through, Robin, would be to file a report with the police and then bolt for home as fast as you could."

She stared at him mutely.

Michael turned to face the front again, adding, "So before you go on questioning me, why don't you explain just who and what you are."

Robin was shaken, angry—and defensive. But she could hardly defend herself, because he was right. Stiffly she said, "I'm a freelance reporter. I usually work the police beat. And I came down here after a story."

He nodded, seeming unsurprised. "I see. A story on white slavery, I suppose."

"Yes. It all started when a friend of mine introduced me to a girl who'd been kidnapped and had managed to get away." Reluctantly Robin added, "And she'd done pretty much what you said, except that she didn't report it to the police. She was too scared; she just ran for home. But she talked to me. She told me about the club she'd gone to—it's the Serendipity, by the way. I thought there was a story, so I came looking."

"Alone?"

Robin hesitated, then replied, "I sent the information to a friend and told her to take it to the police if she didn't hear from me in three days."

"How long ago was that?"

"She would have received the packet three days ago."

Michael half closed his eyes. "Great."

Robin felt defensive again. "Look, I wanted some insurance. If I hadn't managed to get away—"

"I know, I know." He sighed. "It was a smart move. As far as it went."

"I can call Teddy," Robin said, "and let her know I'm fine. Then we can—" She broke off suddenly, realizing something. "You don't want the police involved in this, do you?"

"Not if I have a choice, no," he admitted, frowning.

She stared at his admittedly handsome profile and frowned herself, beginning to put certain things together as her mind began functioning with something like its normal clarity. "You're looking for someone, aren't you? A woman. That's why you suddenly agreed to help me."

After a moment he said lightly, "Either I'm slipping, or else you're too perceptive for your own good."

Robin was still grappling with her thoughts. "You didn't show any interest in helping me until I mentioned the other girl on the yacht. The young girl who was crying. Who is she, Michael?"

"How could I know?"

"You think you know. Who is she?" When he didn't answer immediately, Robin said, "I've been honest with you. The least you can do is tell me what you know."

There was a moment of silence, and then Michael said tightly, "All right. There's a chance I know who she is."

"And who might she be?"

"My sister."

Two

On the fifteenth floor of a gleaming high rise in New York City on a fine Saturday morning, a security officer sat at his desk and looked up expectantly as the elevator bell dinged. The first to disembark from the elevator was an extremely large and shaggy Irish wolfhound who ambled over to the desk and displayed an impressive set of canine fangs in an amiable grin.

The security guard kept his poker face, and dutifully wrote in his log the visitor's name and identification badge number, attached to his collar. "Hello, Wizard," the guard murmured.

"Hi, Phil." Fortunately for Phil's sanity, the salutation didn't come from the dog but from his petite, redheaded mistress, who was second out of the elevator.

"Morning, Mrs. Steele," Phil said in greeting, while the wife of Long Enterprises' security chief signed the log herself.

"Teddy, Phil. I've told you and told you to call me Teddy."

"Yes, ma'am."

They both knew he'd go on addressing her formally.

"Are Raven and Kyle here?" Teddy Steele asked the guard.

"Yes, ma'am. In the computer room."

"Thanks, Phil."

He sat watching her and her canine buddy move down the hall, smiling. As far as Phil was concerned, this had always been an enjoyable company to work for, but the fairly recent addition of several wives to the executive floors made it even more so. Not only were they beautiful women, but they had brought a dash of the unexpected into Long Enterprises. To Phil's mind, they didn't seem to typify executive wives, but since their husbands weren't typical executives, that just made things all the more interesting.

You just never knew, Phil reflected happily, what these interesting people were going to be up to next. . . .

Teddy went into the huge computer room with its massive central brain and data base, which was currently deserted except for two other women at a worktable near the floor-to-ceiling windows. The woman nearest Teddy was tall and lovely with sable hair and vivid blue-green eyes; the wife of Lucas, Long Enterprises' chief investigator, Kyle Kendrick possessed the aristocratic features and background of a society deb and the courage and daring of a stuntwoman. She was also enormously intelligent.

The second woman, also tall, had blue-black hair

and merry violet eyes, was striking rather than beautiful, and was perfectly capable, in her husband's absence, of running the worldwide financial empire that was Long Enterprises. She was also nerveless, daring, smart, and quite experienced in walking the dark side of the streets. She was Raven Long, wife of Josh Long, and currently in charge of her husband's empire.

"Hi," Teddy offered, signaling with her hand for her canine pal Wizard to lie down.

"Hi yourself," Kyle responded, smiling. "What's up?"

"I've got a problem," Teddy told them.

Raven grinned at her. "Don't tell me. Zach heard—somehow—that you went with us to that diplomatic bash last night and is having a long-distance fit."

"I wouldn't be surprised if he heard. The man has built-in radar that never fails to tell him when I'm being 'stubborn' by sticking my head out a window without a bulletproof shield. Honestly! Besides, if he *does* find out, I can argue there were more guards in that place than you could find in Fort Knox."

"Well," Raven said reasonably, "with the guys all out of the country, they're bound to worry. Somebody had to stay and mind the castle, and they could hardly expect us to pull up the drawbridge and flood that moat while they're gone."

"I just wish they'd find out something," Kyle said, frowning a little. "No enemy would go to all the trouble of testing the company's security without following through." She shook her head and, since there was nothing any of them could do about the fact that all three of their husbands were busy searching for a faceless enemy hiding in shadows, she tried to stop thinking about it.

"They'll be all right," Raven said, and if the words were calm and certain, her voice might have wavered just a bit. Of them all, Raven had the most experience of the darker side of life—and of the darker side of human nature; in addition, she had the added burden of knowing it was Josh their faceless enemy had targeted.

"Of course they will," Teddy said, having implicit faith in all their men.

Raven smiled quickly. "With the office pretty much closed for the weekend and no business crises in the offing, we have too much time to brood. We need something to occupy our minds. So . . ." She looked at Teddy. "What's your problem?"

From her huge and rather overstuffed shoulder bag, Teddy unearthed a large manila envelope. "A friend of mine from San Francisco sent me this three days ago," she told them, and began spreading papers out on the worktable.

Raven's merry eyes went grim as she studied the papers, and after she'd read the handwritten note attached, she looked at Teddy with a sober expression. "You haven't heard from her, I take it?"

"No. Not a word."

"Background," Raven requested, and Kyle looked up from the papers attentively.

Teddy put her shoulder bag aside and lifted herself up to sit on the worktable. "Robin and I grew up in the same neighborhood," she told them. "She comes from a long line of cops; her father's been the head of some kind of domestic intelligence organization for about ten years now. It's very hush-hush; I wasn't supposed to know about it, but girls talk."

Raven smiled suddenly. "Ah. Now I see where those 'connections' of yours come from."

Kyle, remembering also, said, "Right. When Kelsey was in trouble in Pinnacle, Teddy got the floor plan of that plant."

Teddy nodded. "I called Daniel Stuart, Robin's father, and he got the floor plan for me."

"A nice friend to have," Raven noted. "Go on about Robin."

"Robin always wanted to be a cop," Teddy said. "From the time we were kids, that was her one and only ambition. And she's always had the nerve of a burglar. I mean, she'd do anything on a dare, and she wasn't afraid of anything that walked, talked, or dug holes."

Raven and Kyle laughed.

"Some pretty mean beasts dig holes," Teddy assured them solemnly.

"You'd know," Kyle murmured, referring to Teddy's affinity with animals of all shapes and sizes.

Teddy grinned. "Anyway, we all expected Robin to join her father, brothers, uncles, and God knows how many other relatives in becoming some kind of cop. She was the only girl in the family with that ambition, by the way. She was taught from infancy to handle guns, and she knew the police handbook verbatim. So . . . she was accepted into the police academy."

"And?" Raven prompted.

"She failed the written exam. Twice. Nobody who knew her could believe it. Not only is she as smart as a whip, but she *knew* that stuff."

Slowly Raven said, "Maybe she didn't want to become a cop. I mean inside, where it counts."

Teddy shrugged helplessly. "I don't know; she wouldn't say a word about it to me. The next thing I knew, she'd cut all ties with her family, moved to the other side of the city, and become a freelance reporter—covering, of all things, the police beat. I know a homicide detective in that area, and when I called him last night, he said Robin has the reputation of being not only fearless, but reckless. He says she'll go anywhere to get a story, and that she has the nose of a cop."

"Have you called her father?" Kyle asked.

Teddy shook her head. "As a last resort, I will. I don't think Robin's even seen him in several years. Daniel isn't the kind of father to push; when she made it clear she was on her own, he gave her the space. But I know he's been worried about her. He seems to think that Robin feels she's failed him somehow."

"By not becoming a cop?" Raven asked.

"I guess. The point is, though, that she's wrong about that. Daniel doesn't care what career she picks as long as she's happy. And she always adored him; he raised her after her mother died fifteen years ago. To cut herself off from him so completely had to be like cutting off an arm."

Kyle, who was still virtually estranged from her own parents, spoke slowly. "Generally we see only the outward trappings of a relationship; it's hard to know what really goes on. No matter how he feels, if Robin's certain she disappointed him by twice failing a test she should have passed, it could have hit her awfully hard. That kind of failure can mark you for life."

Teddy sighed. "All I know for sure is that she's in

trouble, and I'm the one she trusted. I have to do something."

Raven picked up several of the papers on the work-table and leafed through them slowly. "She did her homework," she noted thoughtfully. "Even before she went to Miami, she'd gotten plenty of information on the Serendipity, the owner, and most of the staff." She looked up suddenly. "Is she attractive, Teddy?"

"Beautiful," Teddy answered. "And she has the kind of coloring those white slavers reputedly love: auburn hair and green eyes. You think she's learning about slavery from inside it?"

"I think I wouldn't bet against the possibility," Raven said soberly.

Kyle said, "Let me have the names connected with that nightclub. It doesn't look as if Robin ran them through to NCIC; maybe the Crime Information Center will have something."

Raven handed over the papers and they watched Kyle move to a computer console and begin working. All of them knew how to operate the computers and how to access an almost unlimited variety of data bases; their men had insisted on their having access to as much information as possible in the event of need. And all of them had accepted that need as a definite possibility at any time. Theirs was a dangerous world sometimes.

As they watched their friend work at the computer, Raven said quietly, "After our jaunt down to Kadeira last time, I got Kelsey to tell me all about Captain Siran; he seemed like a good person to know. He's generally in the Miami area, and he works for Hagen only occasionally; officially he's on the payroll of another organization. Maybe he could be our ace. And I have another source down there."

"Oh?"

"Mmm. A man who generally knows what's going on anywhere around Miami, especially if it's illegal. He's helped me out with information from time to time in the past." She looked at her friend. "Assuming we decided to, we could be down there by early afternoon."

Teddy smiled a little. "The guys won't like it," she murmured. "If we go down there, I mean."

"They won't like it," Raven agreed. "But they'll understand."

And that was, after all, the important thing.

Michael Siran was annoyed at himself. He had no business accepting a partner, however temporarily, and especially when that partner seemed to possess just enough knowledge, experience, and anger to make her dangerous. He didn't doubt she had picked up useful information as a reporter, but that hardly qualified her to play police officer or detective.

And Michael was also annoyed at his own inclination to trust her, to talk to her. *That* was a fine trait to develop in his work, a wonderful trait; he'd end up getting himself killed. It was especially galling since he knew without doubt that Robin Stuart was holding out on him. There was something she hadn't chosen to tell him, and he didn't like it.

"How did your sister get herself kidnapped?" Robin was asking him.

"Through no fault of hers," he very nearly snapped.

"She wasn't looking for a hot story three thousand miles from home."

"I didn't mean—" Robin began stiffly.

Michael gestured abruptly, cutting her off. "Never mind. I'm sorry I said that." *Damn. Now I'm apologizing!* He glanced aside to find Robin looking at him with the most beautiful pair of green eyes he'd ever seen, and hastily turned his gaze forward again. This wasn't going to work, it wasn't going to work one bit, he couldn't even keep his mind on—

"She'll be all right," Robin said, obviously trying to reassure him. "They won't hurt her. At least . . ."

"At least not badly?" he finished in a grim tone. "My sister's in a different position from the other girls, Robin. Lisa wasn't snatched for sale to the highest bidder. She was taken to use as bait."

After a moment Robin said slowly, "Bait . . . to catch you?"

"To catch me," he affirmed.

"Then you know who has her?"

"In a manner of speaking." Inwardly cursing himself for telling her all this, he heard himself go on. "I've made a few bad enemies, but there was one in particular. Because of some work I did a few years ago, this man was exiled from his own country. He swore he'd get even, swore he'd steal what I cared about the most."

"Your sister."

"Yes. Lisa."

"If you knew he might try to get his hands on her—"

"Why didn't I do something to prevent it?" Michael felt, as always, a tightening inside at that question, a surge of emotion that was compounded of fear for Lisa and disgust with himself. "I thought I had," he said finally, roughly. "I put her in an extremely private boarding school in Europe three years ago, and she's had special security around the clock. An army couldn't have gotten to her. But Sutton did."

"Edward Sutton?" Robin nearly flinched as steely gray eyes fixed on her.

"You know him?" Michael asked softly.

Robin cleared her throat. "His was one of the names I got while I was nosing around the Serendipity."

"Connected to the club?"

"Very loosely, according to what I heard. There was a hint he was more strongly connected to the illegal gambling going on in the back room."

"Did you ever see him? At the club or on the yacht?"

Robin shook her head. "Not that I know of. Certainly not on the yacht."

Michael was silent for a moment, piloting the boat automatically, his mind working hard. He kept his eyes off Robin. "Gambling," he mused softly, almost to himself. "One of Sutton's hobbies was always high-stakes poker." Abruptly he asked, "Do you know anything about boats?"

"I've crewed on a sailboat the last three summers."

"Good enough. Take the wheel while I change, will you?"

Robin stepped forward to obey, suddenly conscious of the cramped space on the bridge. She caught her breath as he brushed against her but stood gripping the wheel firmly and staring straight ahead. She didn't trust her voice enough to speak.

For a moment, neither did Michael. He had, with

an effort, managed to keep his mind off the lovely body he had stripped naked last night, but the tight confines of the bridge made her closeness and his surge of memories inevitable. She affected him like no woman he'd ever met before, both physically and emotionally. Emotionally, her unusual combination of toughness and vulnerability tugged at something inside him. Physically, he was all too aware of a desire for her more powerful than any he'd felt before, a hunger he could only just control.

His arm still burned from the accidental contact of her breast, and his belly had knotted as if a fist had hit him there. He wanted to reach past her and turn off the engine, allow the boat to drift where it would while he took her below and . . . He shook off the thought with iron control.

"Just keep her on course," Michael muttered, and left.

One of the things Robin knew about herself was that she was generally attracted to very strong men. She knew that—and she didn't like it. At least twice during the past few years she had been briefly involved in relationships that had never gotten off the ground because she had quickly begun to resent the very strength that had first attracted her in a man.

She was afraid it was happening again, and it couldn't have been at a worse time. She didn't have the emotional energy for it, even assuming Michael became attracted to her.

"Another hero," she muttered between gritted teeth, reminding herself. "He saved your life in the best tradition of heroes, and now he's going to help you bury the bad guys. Great. Just great. Give him a medal, but don't, for God's sake, give him . . ." *Your heart.*

It was a good piece of advice. Robin just hoped she could accept it.

As the boat began nearing Miami, traffic on the water increased, and she forced herself to concentrate. She watched the course steadily and began drawing tight all the threads of self-control she could muster. She was afraid she'd need every edge she could get.

Michael hesitated just outside the bridge when he returned, watching her while she couldn't see him. She was handling the boat well, and he wasn't concerned about that. What he was concerned about was his own willingness to involve her in a situation that promised to become even more dangerous before it was over. If he had any sense to all, he reminded himself, he'd make sure she remained in Miami when his boat headed back out to sea, probably on tomorrow morning's tide. But he was somehow reluctant to abandon her.

She had very likely been on the same yacht with Lisa; she had gone through much the same thing as Lisa; she was a link to Lisa. And that was all there was to it, he firmly told himself, and it accounted for his feeling that he couldn't abandon her.

She turned her head suddenly to look at him, green eyes vivid but shuttered against the creamy pale complexion of a true redhead, and he knew he was lying to himself. He wanted Robin, and that had nothing to do with Lisa. This was inside himself, a heavy ache that intensified with every passing hour.

And he didn't know how long he would be able to ignore it.

"How long have you been there?" she asked, sounding rattled.

"Just got here." He stepped inside to take the wheel, consciously trying to avoid touching her—and in consequence touching her all too firmly. She moved a bit awkwardly to get hastily past him, and he heard a muttered "dammit" as she passed with her head bent.

She felt it too, he realized, and that understanding made it more difficult than ever for him to control his desire.

Michael took the wheel and said suddenly, "Look, Robin, this isn't just a fun game you seem willing to play, and if you're with me, you're as much a target as I am. If Sutton gets one look at me, we're both probably dead."

Robin ignored that. She had taken in his change of clothing, noting the faded jeans and the T-shirt he now wore under his windbreaker. With forced calm she said, "If we're going ashore in Miami, I haven't any shoes."

He hesitated, then shrugged with a resigned sigh. "Go below and look in the locker by the cabin door. I think Lisa left a pair of running shoes and a windbreaker the last time she was aboard during her school vacation."

Robin escaped, thankful on two counts: that he wasn't, apparently, going to order her to stay aboard once they were in the marina, and that she'd managed to utter a coherent sentence while her heart was still pounding from an unexpected and somewhat shocking physical reaction to him.

She stood out on deck for a few moments to allow the breeze to cool her hot cheeks, urging herself to overcome this idiotic obsession with strong men before it destroyed her. Then she squared her shoulders and went below, emerging a little while later wearing a black windbreaker and running shoes.

As she returned to the bridge, she spoke instantly, reluctant to allow any silence in which to think idiotic thoughts. "Did you say there was someone you needed to see in the city?"

Michael didn't look at her, but he nodded. "I've changed my mind about who, though," he told her. "If Sutton's still playing high-stakes poker, I know someone who just might have played against him."

"How could that help us?"

"The name of Sutton's yacht, if we're lucky."

Robin frowned, trying to think. "But if you have contacts with any law enforcement officials, they could get the name of the yacht." Then, before he could respond, she added, "Oh—no police. Right?"

"Partly right. No police. But anyway, it's doubtful Sutton registered the yacht in his own name. Extremely doubtful. Chances are, the police have no idea it's his. Sutton's a wanted man, and he wouldn't take a risk that stupid."

"So the police couldn't help. But how would this friend of yours know the yacht's name?"

Michael smiled slightly. "If I know Dane, he probably lost the yacht to Sutton in a poker game."

Robin blinked. "Really? I thought things like that only happened in the movies."

"With Dane, things like that happen every Saturday night. It's not always yachts, of course." He looked reflective. "I haven't seen him in a couple of years. The count must be up to three or four by now."

"What are we counting?"

"Fortunes. Dane's made and spent several by now. 'Made' being a term not to be confused with 'earned.' "

Robin thought about that. "He didn't earn his fortunes? Then how did he get them?"

"Won part of them. Probably stole the rest; I've always suspected he's a first-class cat burglar."

Robin thought about that. "Does this friend of yours help the police from time to time?"

Michael's smile widened. "Dane goes his own way. However, the intelligence community in this country is a relatively small one, and since Dane has the unique ability to unearth skeletons from locked closets, he sometimes has information available to certain interested parties."

"Like yourself?"

"He's never been able to beat me at poker. And I always cut a higher card. For some reason known best to himself, that makes him indebted to me."

Robin was growing more and more amused. "He doesn't sound like a garden-variety informant."

"No. Oh, no. Dane's one of a kind. A hundred or so years ago he would have been a pirate. Go back further, and he would have been a king."

"So in the modern day world he's a gambler."

"That's one facet. An occasional word dropped in the right place is another. Maybe he's a cat burglar.

Maybe not. Maybe he's rich today, or maybe he's shooting craps for his next meal. With Dane, you just never know for sure."

It appeared that Dane was having an off week. They found him after several hours of Michael questioning some of the shadiest-looking people Robin had ever seen in the seediest part of the city. She watched it all with interested eyes, sticking close to Michael and keeping quiet. She was propositioned twice by passersby, both "gentlemen" retreating hastily after one hard look from Michael; she finally zipped up her windbreaker to hide the lack of a bra, adopted a slouch, and tried to go unnoticed.

"It isn't working," Michael told her as they moved purposefully down the crowded sidewalk.

"What?"

He took her hand to guide her around a finely dressed pimp with an interested look on his face. Calmly Michael said, "Your attempt to look less attractive. So far I've had four offers for you. It must be those legs."

She glanced down at her long, bare legs, and swore softly. "I can't help that," she muttered. "The shorts were all I could find." Then, despite herself, she asked curiously, "What did they offer?"

Solemnly he replied, "The best was forty percent of your future income."

Robin didn't know whether to laugh or swear. In the end she just shook her head, glancing aside at Michael to find him smiling a little. Highly conscious of his large, strong hand firmly holding hers, she hastily changed the subject. "Did you find out where Dane is?"

Michael turned them right suddenly into an alley. "Here. I hope." He led her down the dark alley for some twenty yards, then stopped at a battered wooden door that was the only opening in a sad brick wall.

Robin looked at it doubtfully. "Do we knock?"

"No. They'd think it was a raid."

She found herself giggling nervously but followed close behind as Michael released her hand, yanked the warped door open, and entered. They were in what looked like a cluttered storage room with boxes piled high, and made their way to a doorway that led to a dark, narrow hall.

After that Robin lost track of direction in a maze of hallways, all dark and empty. They climbed two flights of stairs and finally wound up at the end of yet another dark hallway and before another warped wooden door. This time Michael knocked with what was obviously a rhythmical signal.

There were several moments of silence, and it wasn't until Robin felt the unsettling sensation of being watched that she noticed the tiny peephole in the door. When the door was audibly unlocked and pulled open, she followed Michael into what felt distinctly like a set for a grade B movie.

It was a small room, thick with cigarette and cigar smoke, and dark except for the single shaded light hanging low over a round table in the center. Half a dozen men were grouped around the table seated in folding chairs, all in their shirt-sleeves. With the exception of one younger man, they were middle-aged. There was a profusion of glittering diamond rings, unidentifiable drinks in thick tumblers, and several overflowing ashtrays.

There was also a pile of money in the center of the table, and none of the bills was less than a hundred.

The man who had let them in relocked the door in silence and returned to the table, and out of the dimness surrounding the low circle of light a deep, beautiful voice spoke sadly.

"Michael, your timing is lousy."

Robin couldn't see the man's face very well from where she was standing beside Michael, but she thought he was younger than the rest, and he was exquisitely dressed in white trousers and vest and neatly knotted tie. He was in his shirt-sleeves, with his suit jacket over the back of his chair, and his hands were beautifully long-fingered and graceful holding the cards.

"Finish the hand," Michael said. "Then we have to talk, Dane."

Robin stood beside him in the shadows near the wall, listening silently as the men continued playing, talking in low voices as the pile of money in the center of the table grew. It was another half hour before the hand finally ended, and it had come down to just two players: Dane and an unnamed man with about six diamond rings and a harsh voice.

"Four of a kind," the harsh voice said, laying down four nines.

There was a beat of silence, and then Dane sighed and stacked his cards neatly facedown before him. "My luck," he said mournfully, "seems to have deserted me today."

With no sign of triumph the winner raked in his money, and the other men gathered their belongings. In a loose group they moved to the door, escorted by Dane, and within moments were gone. Dane crossed the room and snapped up the three shades at the windows and the small room was abruptly flooded with light.

"It better be important," he said cheerfully to Michael.

Robin made her way to the table and sank down in the chair Dane had recently vacated, staring at him. He was a man women would always stare at, she acknowledged silently to herself, feeling a bit numb. He was absurdly young to have made and lost several fortunes, being somewhere in his mid-thirties, and . . . God, the man was *beautiful.*

His size alone made him impressive, since he was easily six and a half feet tall with shoulders to match, and he was lean-waisted and slim-hipped. He looked athletic yet moved with lazy grace as if he couldn't be bothered to stir himself enough to move quickly. His thick, shining hair was black as a raven's wing. And in a lean, tanned face with every feature perfect, his eyes were a striking violet. Robin had never before seen such laughing eyes so vividly filled with life.

"It is important," Michael was saying, taking a seat to Robin's left and watching the other man sit across from him. "This is Robin Stuart. Robin, Dane Prescott."

"Hello, Robin," Dane said.

"Hi," she managed weakly, and tore her gaze away to look down at the cards he had left stacked on the table. She picked up the cards and looked at them, but she had only a moment before he took them from her gently and smoothly as he was gathering the rest from the table.

"What's up?" he asked Michael.

"Ever play cards with Edward Sutton?"

Dane shuffled the deck idly, looking at Michael with a slight smile. Without speaking, he placed the deck facedown between them. Michael reached out and cut the cards, producing the king of spades faceup. Dane cut and got a jack. He sighed.

"Yeah, I've played against him. A number of times."

"At the Serendipity?"

"There. And other places."

Michael glanced at Robin, then said slowly, "We're looking for a yacht we have reason to believe Sutton owns."

Dane grinned. "I called her *Lady Luck.* He changed the name, of course. She'd the *Dragon Lady* now."

"Any idea where she is?"

"No. I might know who to ask, though. Why? What's your interest?"

"Personal."

Dane lifted an eyebrow and waited.

"Did you know he was into white slavery?" Michael asked.

The laughter in Dane's eyes vanished, and his slight smile disappeared. "No. Are you sure about that?"

"Ask Robin."

Robin squarely met Dane's inquiring gaze, still admiring his looks but glad to feel no tug of attraction. "I was at the Serendipity a few nights ago. I had one drink, and there was something in it. I woke up to find myself with four other girls in the cabin of a boat, a yacht. They kept us drugged most of the time, but I managed to get out and jump overboard sometime last night. Michael pulled me out of the water."

"Sure it was Sutton's yacht?" Dane asked.

Michael replied, "Robin's a reporter, and she came up with Sutton's name in connection with that club.

I know he's in the area because he's waiting for me to contact him; he's set a trap for me."

"What's the bait?"

"Lisa."

Dane said something violent under his breath, and though she only half heard what he said, Robin wasn't about to ask him to repeat it.

Michael went on steadily. "Robin heard another girl on the yacht, crying. It's the only lead I've got, Dane."

Immediately Dane said, "There's a man who might know where the *Dragon Lady* is. Big man, with a full beard and about half his teeth. Peculiar man, very dangerous. He's a smuggler. They call him Jack, and only God is privy to what his real name is. He knows the waters around here like the back of his hand, and if anyone has illegal cargo, he'd know about it. He spends his evenings in a dive called the Gold Coast. Watch yourself in there. And don't play cards."

"Why?"

"They shoot the winner."

Michael smiled faintly. "Thanks, Dane."

"Say hello to Lisa for me."

A little while later, as they left the building, Robin said, "I looked at his cards, Michael. Dane had a straight flush, ace high. He won that last hand."

Michael didn't seem surprised. "Did he?"

"And there must have been fifty thousand dollars in that pot." She was bewildered. "Why would he pretend to lose?"

"I'm sure he had his reasons."

"What reason would he have to throw away all that money?"

Michael took her hand as they emerged from the alley. "I know the Gold Coast; they don't even open until after six. Why don't we find a decent restaurant—if we can around here—and get something to eat. You must be starved."

Robin ignored a sudden pang of hunger. "You didn't answer my question," she insisted.

He kept them moving but said dryly, "Dane's probably setting up the man who was wearing all the diamond rings, Robin. And since he can't hide his skill with cards, he just fakes a run of bad luck. It's an old gambler's trick. The mark wins a lot of money in the first few games and feels confident enough to keep playing; then Dane arranges one final game for huge stakes, saying he wants to try to win back what he's lost. And he does."

"Does Dane cheat?" she asked, disliking the thought.

"He doesn't have to. He was probably playing poker in his crib, and he's the luckiest man I know."

"But you said he'd already lost several fortunes."

"Sure. Lost, spent . . . and enjoyed. Dane may sometimes be down, but he's never out. His luck always returns. Now, are you hungry?"

"Starving," she admitted.

Three

They ended up finding a restaurant in a better area of the city, and Robin used the time before their meal arrived to place a call to New York to Teddy's private number first, then the number of Long Enterprises, and drew a blank both times. There was no answer at Teddy's home, and the voice answering the company's phone merely reported that Mrs. Steele was out of town.

Robin, remembering Teddy's impulsiveness, winced as she hung up the receiver. Her childhood friend, she reflected anxiously, was entirely likely to appoint herself the cavalry and come charging to the rescue. And from what Robin had heard and read of the group of people surrounding Joshua Long, a group that included Teddy and her husband, Zach, none of them would be inclined merely to report Robin's disappearance to the police.

Worried, Robin returned to the table where Michael waited.

"Well?" he asked.

"No good. She isn't home, and when I called the company—"

"What company?"

"Long Enterprises. Teddy's husband, Zach, is security chief."

Michael was staring at her, frowning a little. Then the frown faded, and he shook his head. "Those people," he murmured in a voice that was half amused and half worried.

"You know them?" Robin asked in surprise.

"I've . . . well, I've encountered them, let's say. They keep turning up in these kinds of situations. Is your friend like the others? I mean, the type to come down here and investigate rather than call the police?"

"I'm afraid so," Robin confirmed. "But she might not have gotten the package I sent. The switchboard operator at the company just said she was out of town; she may have been gone for days or weeks."

"But she may well be on her way down here."

Robin sighed. "She may, yes." She watched his face intently, a little surprised not to see anger or uneasiness; Michael seemed more thoughtful than anything else, and it was obvious he was thinking hard. "I'm sorry, Michael," she ventured at last.

His gaze focused on her, and he smiled. "Don't worry about it. I don't know your friend, but if she brings any of that crew along with her, they won't blunder in recklessly. They're all too smart, and too careful. I did hear, though . . ."

"Hear what?"

Michael hesitated, then shrugged. "That Josh Long and several of his men had dropped out of sight.

Something's in the wind there, but I don't know what. Still, there's apparently nothing we can do but wait and see who turns up."

"Isn't that awfully risky?"

His smile went crooked. "Awfully." He glanced up as their waitress approached with laden plates, and the conversation was over for the time being.

Robin was as grateful for the distraction of eating as she was for the food itself. During the encounter with Dane, she had managed to keep her mind occupied, but whenever she and Michael were alone she found it more and more difficult to ignore the tug of attraction that seemed to be growing stronger. And it didn't help this time, knowing he was just the kind of man she had always resented. This time, her body and emotions refused to accept reason.

She caught herself stealing glances at him, grateful that he seemed preoccupied and unaware of her attention. She felt curiously, unusually, helpless, unable to fight this. As if something inside her *knew*, without doubt, that it was inevitable. And so strong was that conviction that Robin felt tense, on the brink, waiting. He hadn't even touched her except casually or by accident, yet her body felt heavy and restless, feverish.

She could keep her mind on the dangerous situation they were involved in, yet just beneath that calm surface something was moving, slowly, like water under ice. And she was very much afraid that the ice would crack, splinter, leaving her changed forever.

Because she hadn't dared return to her hotel, Robin

was without money, and she hadn't been happy about accepting even a meal or change for her phone call from Michael since she already owed him so much. But her somewhat fierce assurances of paying him back were met with grave acceptance, and that eased her mind somewhat.

Still, she couldn't help but feel that theirs was an unequal partnership; more than anything else she wanted to pull her own weight. It was just a few hours later when she got her chance. She and Michael finally had found the tavern Dane told them about.

The bar rejoicing in the name Gold Coast turned out to be just what Dane had called it—a dive. Sandwiched between two pawnshops with heavily barred windows and located on a side street in the worst part of the city, the tavern was dank, dark, filled with smoke, and echoing with the harsh sounds of coarse laughter. There were several rickety tables around which card games were going on; the long wooden bar was stained and splintered; and the bartender boasted the tattoo of a naked woman on one corded forearm and a ship's anchor on the other.

Standing beside Michael outside and peering cautiously through a dirty window, Robin shivered inwardly. The man they had come to see was easily visible at the far end of the bar, and he looked more dangerous than any other man in the room. Just as Dane had described, "Jack" was huge, massive really, heavily bearded, and when he ordered another drink, she could see that several of his teeth were missing.

She could feel Michael tensing even though his

face remained expressionless, and when he began to move toward the door she quickly grabbed his arm. "Wait!" she whispered.

His voice was low as well. "You stay here. And keep in the shadows. If anything happens to me—"

Robin wrapped both hands around his muscled arm and held on grimly. "Michael, you can't go in there. We've been standing here ten minutes, and there have already been three fights. There's no way you can expect to go in there asking suspicious questions and still come out alive!"

He looked down at her, mouth tightening. "What choice do I have, Robin?"

"You're not even armed."

"They'd kill me for sure if I was."

"Wait," she insisted, turning her head to look back into the tavern. "Let me think a minute."

Michael drew a deep breath. "It won't be the first time I've gone into a place like this. I can handle it."

"I'm sure you can," she said almost absently, staring into the tavern with her eyes suddenly narrowed. "But there'd be some kind of fight. You're too dangerous; it shows too plainly. You'd be a threat to them."

"Robin—"

She looked back at him quickly. "We don't want to draw attention to ourselves, do we? That's the last thing we need."

"Agreed. But there isn't a choice."

She lifted her chin and struggled to hide the terror she felt. "Yes, there is. I can go in."

"You?" He laughed shortly.

Robin hoped he was strong enough that he didn't feel a need to prove it with macho stand-back-little-woman-and-let-me-do-it determination. Steadily she said, "I've done something like this before. Please, Michael, trust me. I know what I'm doing. But I'll need a couple of props."

"Props?" He was staring down at her, frowning.

"Yes. That pawnshop over there is still open. Try to find a necklace with a crucifix on it—the bigger the better. And if they have any clothing, get a pair of long pants for me; it'll be better if they don't fit."

He was still frowning a little, but understanding had dawned. "What if it doesn't work, Robin?"

She managed a faint smile. "Then you're the rescue team."

Michael hesitated, but he had a good idea of what she had in mind and there was a chance it would work. If he had been partnered with a female agent on an assignment, he wouldn't have hesitated at all; as it was, he was worried about Robin and uncertain of her abilities. "Are you sure you've done something like this before?" he asked finally.

"Yes. And for the same reason. To get information."

"Wait here," he said, and headed next door to the pawnshop.

Robin closed her eyes briefly and commanded herself to stop shaking. Still, it took a ridiculous amount of time to remove her shoelaces because her hands trembled so. She arranged her long hair in two ponytails and used the laces to tie them just below her ears. Then she bent and rubbed her hands in the dirt that had collected against the building; some of the dirt was also transferred to her face.

Michael reappeared suddenly beside her. "I did my best," he told her, handing over a long silver chain and a bundle of dark cloth.

She put the necklace on, satisfied with the big silver crucifix that showed clearly against her black windbreaker. Then she stepped into the dark pants and pulled them up over her shorts; they were too long and the waist was far too loose, but the baggy appearance was what she'd wanted.

"How do I look?" she asked, gazing up at him.

Michael had an odd expression on his face, and his voice had rough edges. "Like the littlest hobo. Robin—"

"Good," she said, cutting him off. "I'll try to be as quick as I can." She hoped desperately that he couldn't see her fear.

He bent his head suddenly and kissed her, briefly but firmly. "Be careful," he urged.

Robin found herself at the door without being aware of moving, thinking vaguely that it wasn't at all fair of him to have done that just when she needed all her wits about her. Then she took a deep breath and went into the tavern.

Michael waited tensely by the window, never taking his eyes off the scene inside. He could feel as well as see all conversation and activity cease when she walked in, and he silently approved the timid way she glanced around. With the baggy clothing and hairstyle she looked about twelve years old, and it was clear that appearance made the men doubtful enough to do nothing while she walked slowly to the end of the bar where Jack sat.

Tensing even more now, Michael almost held his breath as the big man looked at Robin. She must have said something, for Jack nodded and she climbed up on the stool beside him, sitting with hunched shoulders and a hesitant tilt to her head.

Immediately the crowd of men seemed to lose interest, and returned to their former activities.

Michael found himself smiling in admiration. By God, she'd done it! Now if she only could get the information and get out of there in one piece.

Robin had never been so terrified in her life. It hadn't even been this bad when she had woken up to find herself in the possession of white slavers. And she knew why, of course. Because this time someone was counting on her to get the job done. This time someone else expected her to be strong.

"Who sent you to me?" Jack asked her in a rumbling voice.

She fixed her gaze on the big gold crucifix he was wearing, and didn't have to try to make her voice timid and shaky. "I think he said his name was Dane. He said you might be able to tell me where I could find the *Dragon Lady.*"

"Whatcha want with that tub, kid?"

Inventing as she went along, Robin answered softly. "Mr. Sutton offered me a job a while back. I need to talk to him."

Jack was chewing on the stub of a cigar, his eyes narrowed against the rising curl of smoke as he stared at her. With a short laugh he said, "You don't want no job that bastard offers you, girl. Do yourself a favor and forget the idea."

With a facility that had been hers since childhood, Robin allowed tears to form in her eyes, and let her voice quaver. "I have to find that boat. Eddie works on that boat, and I have to find him."

"You don't look old enough to have an Eddie,"

Jack said, but in the world-weary tone that expected budding adolescents to have dangerous boyfriends. "In trouble, eh?"

Robin let her eyes skitter away from his. "I have to find Eddie," she repeated dolefully.

Jack sighed and shifted the cigar to the other side of his mouth. "Girl, Sutton's carrying valuable cargo, and he ain't going to want no crying girlfriend pestering one of his men."

"I won't pester him," she said, allowing hope to creep into her voice. "I'll just stand by and wait till Eddie's shift ends. Unless . . . they're at sea?"

Jack grunted in brief amusement. "None of us are at sea with the waters boiling like they're from hell," he muttered.

Robin didn't react to his awareness of the law enforcement activity all around the coast but merely looked at him with a spaniellike expression. "Please tell me where the boat is," she begged.

Almost angrily he said, "It's no skin off my nose if you want to get your silly ass shot off. Sutton usually anchors in a cove off one of the Ten Thousand Islands. They call that island the Maze, and for good reason."

"Thank you," Robin said breathily, sliding off the stool.

"Here." He reached out suddenly and stuffed something into one of the pockets of her windbreaker. "Hop a bus back to Iowa, or wherever you're from. Now, get outta here."

She nodded and moved quickly back to the door, relieved to find no further attention paid her by the men in the tavern. Immediately outside the door Michael took her hand and drew her into the shadows.

"Anything?" he asked.

His hand felt very warm, and Robin knew her own was ice cold. "Yes," she murmured, trying to get the shake out of her voice. "An island in the Ten Thousand group. It's called the Maze. He said Sutton usually anchors in a cove there."

"I know where it is. Good work," Michael said sincerely, then asked, "What's that?"

Robin was staring in astonishment at two hundred-dollar bills she had pulled from her pocket. "He—he gave me this. Told me to get a bus back to wherever I was from."

Michael grinned a little. "What line did you give him?"

"I said I was looking for my boyfriend, that he worked on Sutton's yacht. He, that is, Jack assumed I was pregnant."

Still holding her hand, Michael began moving away from the tavern. "You must have touched his soft spot if he gave you two bills," he said philosophically.

"I can't keep the money!" she protested.

"You'll have to. It wouldn't be in character to give it back. Besides, do you really want to go back in there?"

"No. But it isn't right."

Patiently Michael said, "Then we'll stop at a church somewhere and you can put it in the collection box."

Robin sighed but walked beside him without further protest. She knew she was stupid to feel guilty at accepting money from a man like Jack under false pretenses; it was probably ill-gotten gains anyway. Still, he'd been kind to her in a rough way, and she couldn't help but feel bad about it.

"How did you guess they wouldn't bother you in there?" Michael asked curiously as they walked.

"It made sense." He seemed to have forgotten he was still holding her hand, and Robin wondered why she didn't pull it away. "A girl dressed like I am, probably pretty young and down on her luck—but wearing a religious medal she could have pawned. A cop told me once that some of the roughest men still have a tendency to respect 'good' girls. I took the chance."

"You sure did." He squeezed her hand briefly. "And you pulled it off. You've got guts, I'll give you that."

Still fooling them all! Robin's bitterness grew when she realized that the aftermath of fear had left her feeling weak and shaky—as always. Oh, damn, why couldn't she conquer her fear? Why couldn't she find some hint of courage inside herself?

"Thanks," she said tautly, and immediately changed the subject because she felt like a fraud. "Are we going back to the boat?"

"After we stop for supplies, I think we'd better. And we should head for that island right away. The crackdown on boats in these waters won't last more than a couple more days, I'd guess. Once the heat's off, Sutton could decide to bolt."

For the first time, Robin wondered what he planned to do when they found the yacht. If Sutton was indeed on old enemy, then Lisa's position was decidedly precarious. From what Robin had heard, Sutton was just as likely to enter into a gun battle with a Coast Guard vessel as he was to surrender to them.

In a small voice she said, "We can't just tip off the Coast Guard about that yacht, can we?"

After a moment Michael said, "I don't know, but it's doubtful. One hint of trouble, and Sutton's likely to throw the girls overboard. And they won't be in any condition to survive that."

"Then how can we help them? How can we get them and Lisa off the boat safely?"

"I don't know, Robin." Michael walked on steadily, not looking at her. "I just don't know."

It wasn't over, Robin realized, going cold inside again. The worst wasn't over. She'd had some vague idea of alerting the proper officials and standing by while the girls and Michael's sister were safely rescued. But she realized now that it wouldn't be so easy, or so simple. Finding the yacht wouldn't be enough.

She forced her voice to remain steady. "We'll need some kind of backup once we find the yacht."

As they turned in the direction of the marina, Michael stopped suddenly and faced her. They stood before a tavern slightly more upscale than the one Robin had gone into, and the hellish glow of a red neon sign in the window lit Michael's face and made his grim expression all too obvious.

"No, Robin."

"There must be someone you can trust!"

"That isn't the point."

"Yes, it is," Robin insisted, and felt a flash of bitterness spurred as much by her own self-doubts as anything else. "But it has to be you, right? Just you alone, and never mind that you're way the hell outnumbered."

"Robin—"

The ice was cracking, and fear was the reason. Fear for him. Nothing mattered except this terrible hunger for him, clawing at her until she was raw and helpless. He'd get himself killed, and every instinct she could lay claim to surged in protest. The feelings tangled inside her in wild confusion.

She jerked her hand away and forced a hard laugh. "I hate heroes, I really do. They make the rest of us feel so damned inadequate!" Then, horrified to have said that aloud for the first time, she shoved her hands into the pockets of her windbreaker and hurried past him. She knew he was behind her, but he didn't speak and didn't attempt to catch up. Robin was blessed with a good sense of direction, and even with her thoughts and emotions in turmoil was able to find the marina easily.

She found herself alone once she reached the boat, and realized only then that Michael must have stopped somewhere to get those supplies he mentioned. Miserable, she went below and took a shower in the tiny bathroom, making use of the first opportunity she'd had to wash away the salt of her enforced swim of last night. She found another pair of cutoff jeans and a short-sleeve green blouse, then went up on deck to allow her hair to dry in the night breeze.

The marina was well lit, and she saw Michael easily when he returned almost an hour later carrying two boxes of groceries and supplies. He didn't look at her as he jumped aboard and took the stuff below, and Robin felt even more miserable.

Typical Robin, shooting her mouth off, she thought. She'd had no right to say that. He was worried to death about his sister—and he was an agent, for God's sake; of *course* he was courageous enough to deal with Sutton alone. He would too; she knew he would. Heroes, sure. And *she* had to be attracted to them.

Especially attracted to Michael Siran.

Robin groaned inwardly and rested her forehead on her upraised knees. Oh, Lord, she was doing it again! Like ore to a magnet, she couldn't help but give in to the attraction of strong men . . . only to find herself resenting them, because she, a coward, could never feel equal in such a relationship.

That was all it was, of course. All. Just an attraction, and these other tangled feelings didn't mean anything at all. She was a dumb woman with an insane fascination of strong men. Nothing more.

Desperately, she went on lying to herself.

Eyes closed, she felt more than heard soft footsteps on the deck, and became aware that Michael had sat down on the padded bench across from the one she occupied. She heard the snap of a lighter, and looked up to find him lighting a cigarette, face expressionless.

"You want to tell me what that was all about?" he asked when the lighter was back in this pocket.

She cleared away the lump in her throat. "Nothing. It wasn't about anything. I'm sorry; I shouldn't have said it."

"I want to know why you said it, Robin."

"Just forget it, all right?"

"No." He leaned forward, elbows on his knees, and looked at her steadily. "There's something going on inside you that I don't like, something that's tearing you up. So what's this crap about heroes—and your feeling inadequate?"

She stiffened. "It's nothing. I told you."

Michael began frowning. "Robin, I don't know what

you think I am, but if you've got some image of armor and a white charger, you can forget it."

"Not that kind of hero." Robin heard herself, and she couldn't believe she was saying this; she had never told anybody about her stupid fixation. "Not the storybook stuff, all pretty and white and bloodless. The real thing, Michael, that's what you are. You and men like you."

"Robin—"

"Oh, I know all about men like you." She knew her voice was shaking, but the words burst out nonetheless, like waters from floodgates. "My father, my brothers, uncles—all cops. My father. He's a cop like you, the kind of cop you don't read about in the papers. He earns scars instead of medals, just like you do, I'll bet. He hasn't any nerves and doesn't know what fear is. Like you. Pressure never gets to him, and he never doubts himself and his abilities, and he's always in control. Like you."

"Stop it, Robin." Michael suddenly rose and crossed the small deck between them, tossing his cigarette overboard and sitting down on the bench near her raised legs. "Is that what you think a hero is, some kind of superman? Robin, you just described a machine, not a human being. And you sure as hell didn't describe me."

He was too close, too near, and her body was heating slowly. Her laugh was a small, hollow sound. "Didn't I? You're going to tackle Sutton alone even though you'll be outnumbered at least ten to one. What do you call that?"

"My only option." He took a breath, releasing it impatiently. "Robin, if I thought we could get more than ourselves and this boat anywhere near Sutton's yacht unobserved, we'd have an army as backup. I'm not too proud to yell for help, but in *this* situation one man has a better chance of getting on that yacht without raising the alarm."

"And then?" Her voice was taut. "What, Michael? Do you think you can get those girls off the boat by yourself? Or are you going to take a cannon along to persuade all those armed men to give up peacefully?"

"I don't know what I'm going to do yet," he said, more than a suggestion of clenched teeth in his voice. "But I'll do whatever it takes to get Lisa and those other girls safely out of Sutton's hands."

"I know." She tried and failed to smile. "That's what makes you a hero, Michael. That's what fearless men do."

"Fearless?" He laughed shortly. "Fear's an old friend of mine, Robin. And right now I'm shaking inside."

She stared at him, feeling a jolt of shock. All the strong men she had known and none had ever admitted to fear. Granted, she hadn't brought the question up; because they appeared utterly fearless, she had accepted that as truth. But if this man, whose strength and courage she could almost see, like an aura around him, if this man admitted to fear . . .

"It doesn't show," she whispered.

He was still frowning, his sharp gray eyes probing hers. "Of course it doesn't show; I don't let it. Just like you don't let it show."

"It shows on me like a red flag," she told him, stubborn insistence in her voice. "And every time, every time I have to go into a bad situation, every time I have to at least pretend to be strong, the fear eats me up inside. And I know I'll freeze. I'll freeze up, and I'll get someone killed. That's why I couldn't be—" She broke off, horrified.

But it was too late. Michael finished the sentence quietly, a dawning understanding in his expression. "That's why you couldn't be a cop, like your father."

Robin tried to draw away from him, but she was hemmed in by the side of the boat and by the long legs stretched out beside the bench. She couldn't move away without touching him, and suddenly she was more afraid of touching him than of anything else.

"That's it, isn't it, Robin?"

Her arms tightened around her upraised knees, and she couldn't look away from those clear, perceptive eyes. "I went through the academy," she said almost inaudibly. "Everyone said I was born to be a cop. But I knew the truth. I knew I was always afraid. I knew someone would depend on me someday, a partner, and I'd freeze up. I'd be paralyzed with fear, and I'd get that partner, or someone else, killed."

"Did you ever freeze up?" he asked quietly.

"That doesn't matter, don't you see? I knew I would. And I couldn't be a cop when I knew that."

"What happened? Did you drop out of the academy?"

She swallowed hard. "No. I failed the written exam. Twice. I failed it twice."

Michael looked at her for a long moment, then said, "So you stuck that label on yourself as well."

"What label?"

"Failure. Is that what your father called you?"

"No." She avoided his eyes. "I didn't give him the

chance. I haven't seen him in three years. A coward to the end."

"Stop it." He reached out, grasping both her shoulders and holding them hard. "Robin, fear is natural; in a dangerous situation you'd be an idiot if you weren't afraid. And that failure of yours wasn't an honest one."

"I know what I am," she whispered, trying to ignore the hard strength of his chest pressed against her arms.

He seemed about to shake her, but then drew a breath and spoke roughly. "Do you? Well, let me tell you what others know about you, Robin. What *I* know about you, even though we've known each other less than twenty-four hours. I know that you went through an experience that would have destroyed most women. You were kidnapped, drugged, treated like a piece of merchandise. But you still managed to save yourself by getting away and jumping overboard. And then, when any other woman would have run to escape those painful memories, you teamed up with a stranger to try to save those other women.

"You went into a place that half the cops I've ever met would have avoided like the plague, filled with men very like the ones who kidnapped you. And you *did* it, Robin. You instinctively assumed the one role that provided the slight chance of success. And it worked. You went in for information—and you came out with it. You got the job done."

"I was afraid!" she cried.

"So what? You think courage is measured by the lack of fear? No, Robin, it's the opposite. Courage is doing what you have to *despite* fear."

"I don't believe you," she said, thinking of her father, always smiling, confident, unafraid.

Michael did shake her then, but gently. His gray eyes went steely suddenly, with the inward-turned look of self-appraisal. "I've been in this business for ten years," he told her flatly, "and I'm very good at what I do. I've worked in the Middle East, South America, every part of Europe and Asia. Dirty jobs, most of them, and hellishly tangled. I've been betrayed by people I thought were friends, captured, held prisoner. And, Robin . . . I've been *afraid.*"

She stared at him, seeing the naked truth. "But it didn't paralyze you," she whispered. "It didn't stop you."

"No. And it won't stop you. You doubted yourself and your abilities in the beginning, and that's natural. But you seem to keep misinterpreting your own reactions to danger. The point isn't that you're afraid. The point is that it doesn't stop you."

"What if it does one day?"

"It won't."

"How can I be sure of that?"

The hands on her shoulders gentled. "Robin, you should be sure of it now. You've already faced dangers most people never encounter. You just have to accept that fear is two-o'clock-in-the-morning courage."

Feeling very shaken, she murmured, "Is that a quote?"

He smiled a little. "Paraphrase. Look it up sometime. Because that's the kind of courage you have. The rarest kind."

Robin drew a breath, aware suddenly of the quiet of the marina, of the gentle rocking motion of the boat. Of him. His long fingers were moving on her shoulders, almost absently probing; his eyes were darkening. And she couldn't look away from him. She had an abrupt memory of jumping off that yacht, of sinking into dark waters, alone and afraid.

"What is it about you?" he murmured, clearly puzzled. "I've talked more in the last twenty-four hours than I usually do in a month."

"You're . . . very alone, aren't you?"

"Except for Lisa."

Robin shook her head slightly. "That isn't what I meant."

"I know." His eyes were searching her face now, still puzzled, as if he were looking for something. "Professionally I rarely work with a partner. Personally I suppose I never thought it was fair to begin a relationship that couldn't last."

"You mean friendship? Or a lover?"

"Both. My life would strain any kind of relationship."

Robin was trying to concentrate, trying to keep her mind off the slow, inexorable awakening of her body and senses. "But you must have friendships. Dane, for one."

Michael tilted his head slightly, listening. "Maybe it's your voice," he said absently, then responded to her comments before she could react. "Dane? No, Dane isn't a friend. We don't know enough about each other for friendship. I'm secretive; he's enigmatic. He's too good a card player for my peace of mind. And even though I'd trust him with my life— and have in some situations—I'm not so sure I'd turn my back to him."

She felt a sudden pang, remembering what he had said about having been betrayed by those he'd considered friends. "You two seemed to know each other so well. And yet you still feel suspicious?"

One of his hands lifted from her shoulder and brushed a strand of auburn hair from her face, then lingered warmly against her neck. "I've always hedged my bets, Robin," he said quietly. "Because sure things sometimes stumble, and the long shots can get you killed."

"Which am I?" she heard herself ask unsteadily. "The sure thing? Or the long shot?"

"I don't know." His hand slid around to the nape of her neck, and he began drawing her toward him. "But for the first time in my life . . . I don't know if I can hedge this bet."

Against her conscious volition, Robin felt her hands lifting to touch his chest, felt her legs parting so that as he drew her closer she was heavily aware of the warmth of his body in the hollow of her thighs.

"I don't think . . . this is a very good idea," she managed to say almost inaudibly.

"Of course it isn't," he said huskily. "What the hell does that matter?"

Robin forgot her objections the moment his lips touched hers. She forgot everything but him and the violent surge of emotions rushing through her. She had never felt anything like this, and the force of it shocked her. It came from him, that force, but there was an equally strong response from deep inside herself, and that stunned her; she had never before felt such power.

Her arms went up around his neck as he pulled her fiercely against him, and she felt him draw one of her legs across his, stroking the slender thigh left bare by her shorts. With a mind of its own, her body arched into his, driven to be closer.

A wild sound tangled in the back of her throat as his mouth slanted across hers, deepening the kiss, and heat jolted through her like wildfire. What did it matter, she wondered dazedly, that there would have to be a reckoning for this, that she would pay dearly in tattered emotions. What did it matter that this time she was drawn to a man stronger than any she had ever known, with a force of will that would inevitably deepen her own sense of failure.

Nothing mattered except now, this moment, and the feelings he was drawing from her deepest self.

It was Michael who pulled back suddenly, holding her away from him with iron hands on her shoulders. His face was pale except for the hard flush on his cheekbones, his eyes glittering. "I didn't plan on you," he said hoarsely.

Robin was staring at him, dazed. She forced her arms to let go of him. "Oh, damn," she muttered, realizing only then that it was too late for her to fight this. Far too late. "I didn't plan on you either."

He released her and drew away slowly, rising to his feet and staring down at her. His eyes were violent, but his face remained hard and still.

Robin spoke before he could, fighting to hold her voice steady. "You may not know which I am, a sure thing or a long shot, but you know what this is, don't you?" She didn't have to elaborate; he knew that "this" was the explosive attraction between them.

Michael nodded with stark control. "I know. It's a long shot. One chance in a million. And I don't bet on long shots."

She watched him move away and begin preparations to leave the marina, feeling hot and restless. And despite what Michael had said, she was still afraid.

She didn't bet on long shots—usually. And Michael didn't bet on them—usually. But here they were, getting ready to sail off on this small boat alone to try to rescue women being held by armed men on a large yacht.

And if that wasn't a long shot . . . then what was?

Four

In a luxurious condo high above Miami's famous gleaming white strip of beach, Dane Prescott turned away from the bar in the sunken living room and abruptly went still. Seconds passed. His preoccupied frown slowly faded, a smile taking its place.

"For someone who's reputedly out of the business," he murmured to the apparently empty room, "you sure creep around on cat feet. And I've never known a retiree more inclined to pick locks and disable security systems."

"You ought to change that system," Raven Long said, stepping down into the living room. "It's lousy."

"I'm a guest here," Dane told her politely. "The place belongs to a friend."

Raven looked around, then gazed at him with a lifted brow. "Broke this week?" she asked him dryly.

"No. But near enough." He shrugged, dismissing what was obviously an unimportant problem. "What brings you down to sunny Miami? Last I heard, you'd married Joshua Long and had retired from the world of shadows and secrets."

"You know what they say about retired agents. They just can't keep out of the dark. I need some information, Dane."

"Ask away."

"Do you know Michael Siran?"

"Yes. Would you like a drink?"

Raven's eyes narrowed slightly. "Will I be here that long?"

"You might."

"Okay. Brandy."

He poured her drink, then carried it to her and gestured for her to sit down. When she had, he joined her at one end of the plush gold grouping in the center of the room. "Why are you looking for Michael?" he asked.

"I might need his help. A friend of a friend could well be in trouble down here. Very likely is in trouble. She hasn't checked out of her hotel, but her things are still there and she hasn't been seen for the past few days. She's a reporter, and she was looking into a white slavery ring."

Raven studied her brandy thoughtfully. "I'm here with some friends. We checked the marina a couple of hours ago and found we'd just missed Siran's boat. Where is he, Dane?"

"Unless I'm much mistaken," Dane said, "he's with your friend of a friend. If her name's Robin Stuart, that is."

Raven blinked, then smiled. "How did that happen?"

"Seems she wasn't just looking into white slavery; she fell into it. Managed to jump ship in the dead of night. By a great stroke of luck, Michael was in the vicinity. He fished her out of the water."

Raven sighed. "Teddy will be relieved."

"Don't celebrate yet," Dane warned her.

Raven half closed her eyes. "The slavers?"

"Afraid so. Michael and Robin came to see me this afternoon asking about Edward Sutton's yacht. They had a pretty good idea that was the boat Robin escaped from. I'd say it was a case of out-of-the-frying-pan for Robin; she just happened to be rescued by the one man who's capable of—and highly motivated to—put Sutton out of business for good. Sutton's an old enemy of Michael's, and he's holding someone very dear to Michael as bait to draw him out."

"Who?"

"His sister. My guess is that since this is personal to Michael, he's on his own. No backup." Dane shook his head a little. "He'd storm hell if the devil had his sister; that's about what he's doing now. The odds aren't good, Raven."

"Then we'll improve them," she said grimly.

After a moment Dane smiled. "Okay. What do you need from me?"

In his office in a larger East Coast city, Daniel Stuart slowly closed the folder on a surveillance report he had just received from one of his agents. He was frowning, and hesitated for a moment before reaching for his special phone, and dialing a special number. The call would be routed through several area codes before finally reaching the mobile phone at the other end of the connection. It was after midnight. He heard a dozen clicks, then the ring signal. At last, the phone was answered.

"Yeah?" a voice grunted.

"Where are you?" Daniel asked without preamble.

"Too close to home. Miami."

"That's where the ladies went?"

"Three of them. Raven Long, Kyle Kendrick, and Teddy Steele. One of the company jets touched down a few hours ago. And they almost lost me, dammit."

"I did warn you that they sometimes move fast. Any sign of their husbands?"

"No, and I don't think they came down here to join them. The women checked the marina, asking the harbor master about the *Black Angel*."

"Michael's boat?" Frowning, Daniel ran long fingers through his steel-gray hair. "Any idea why?"

"No. But I can find out." There was wry humor in the deep voice. "Raven Long just left the condo where Dane's living at the moment."

Daniel half closed his eyes. "This is getting hellishly complicated, Skye."

"Tell me about it."

"If those ladies have taken off after Michael . . ."

"Yeah. Well, there's something going on, that's for sure. I think the ladies are on their own this time, and they're moving very fast. An interesting surveillance, I'll say that."

"Find out what you can from Dane." Daniel sighed. "And let me know immediately."

"Right."

Daniel cradled his receiver and sat for a moment, thinking. There was no need, he decided, to alert Hagen; it wasn't the women that other federal honcho was interested in. But Daniel felt distinctly uneasy. None knew better than he what Michael was up against, and if those ladies were trying to find him . . .

He stared at the phone, hoping Skye would report in to him *very* soon.

"Why did you name her *Black Angel*?" Robin asked.

Michael, standing at the wheel in the dimly lit bridge, didn't answer immediately. He watched the boat's instruments and gazed ahead into darkness. He hadn't said much since they'd left the marina hours earlier, and Robin had gone below to try to sleep.

But sleep had been impossible, so she had returned, watching him pilot the boat and feeling unsettled. She told herself she should be relieved that he wasn't willing to bet on their long-shot chances of a relationship, but she couldn't help but feel the irrational sting of rejection.

And she felt lonely, needing to hear the sound of his voice. So she tried again. "After the angel of death?"

"That was her name when I bought her," he said finally.

Robin was glad of that, but his answer left her with no reasonably innocuous subject to talk about. He had shut her out with an iron will, and even though she knew why, it didn't lessen the pain she felt. "How long will it take us to get there?" she asked.

"By dawn if we're lucky."

Robin tried to think clearly; if he was hell-bent on doing this alone, then she had to help him all she could. "Does Sutton know what your boat looks like?"

"He probably knows the name and general description."

"Then we can't get near him."

"No," Michael agreed. "But the Maze is close to several other small islands, and the fishing isn't bad there. We shouldn't look too suspicious getting in close enough to spot the yacht."

"And then?"

"There's an inlet on the opposite side of the island from the cove. We can anchor there."

"And then?" she repeated evenly.

Still refusing to look at her, Michael drew a deep breath. "I'm thinking only one step ahead, Robin, and that's all."

"You said you never bet on long shots," she heard herself say. "What else could you call what you're doing?"

"I told you—I don't have a choice."

Robin decided to drop the subject for a while. Leaning against the doorjamb and highly aware of the darkness all around them, she asked as lightly as she could manage, "How did you happen to get involved in this business anyway?"

"Naval intelligence. But I wasn't a career man, and when I got out there were . . . other offers."

"When was that?"

"Eight years ago." He sent her a speaking glance, then looked back ahead and added in a deliberate tone, "Our parents had been killed the year before, and Lisa had been in a boarding school while I finished my tour with the navy. She loved the school and wanted to stay there. It seemed best. I couldn't provide a settled home for her then, and it wasn't likely that state of affairs would change since I've never been suited for a nine-to-five desk job. But I've always been able to take time off for her vacations and holidays."

"How old is Lisa now?"

"Sixteen."

"Does she know what you do?"

Michael nodded slightly. "She's had to. Not when she was younger, of course, but I told her four or five years ago. I wanted her to know she'd be taken care of . . . if something happened to me."

Robin was silent.

He sent her another look, and his voice grated. "I did my best."

Without thinking, Robin reached out to touch his arm briefly. "I know you did. I was just remembering how I felt when my father told me he'd gone into intelligence work. It was ten years ago, and I was eighteen. It had been easy to accept the danger of his being a cop because I'd grown up with it. And my brothers had become cops. But intelligence . . . I understand what that meant. Even though he said he wouldn't be a field agent, I knew him too well to believe it."

"Does he head up an agency?" Michael asked slowly.

"Yes. I don't know what it's called. But it's one of those small agencies formed during the last fifteen years to help regular law enforcement agencies cope with all the craziness in the world today—drugs, terrorists, international crime rings. All of that."

"Where's it based?"

Robin looked at him curiously. "I couldn't say. For a few years Dad was mostly on the West Coast. After that he seemed to be fairly . . . mobile. And I haven't seen him in three years." When Michael said nothing, she reverted to the original topic. "Lisa must be very strong."

"Yes. But she shouldn't have to cope with my enemies."

"There was nothing you could have done to prevent it, Michael. You know that."

"She deserves a normal life."

"What's a normal life?" Robin shook her head slightly. "Normal is what you get accustomed to."

"I suppose," he answered, but there was no conviction in his voice.

She studied him in silence for a moment. The glow from the boat's instruments cast a blue aura about him, throwing his features into stark relief. He looked a hard, grim man, a dangerous man. But she was beginning to realize that the man inside was different.

An innately quiet and reflective man, his abilities and background had led him into a dangerous world. He had learned to be wary, to never bet on long shots. He had learned to trust no one completely, to weigh every word, to measure the reach of every outstretched hand offering help. The bitterness of betrayals was buried inside him, as well as the pain of failures.

She knew all of that. And she was beginning to realize her lifelong conception of "heroes" had been built on a number of misconceptions. She was just starting to understand that heroes, like all men, felt tired, and discouraged, and afraid. That heroes sometimes failed, and sometimes hesitated, and sometimes made the wrong decisions. That they were human.

It was a jolt to Robin in more ways than one. As long as she'd thought of heroes as larger than life, as fearless beings, she could distance herself, using the buffer of her own feelings of inadequacy. But now the buffer was vanishing.

Always before, when helplessly attracted to a strong man, Robin had been able to withdraw by rousing resentment, by assuring herself she could never hope to be equal; that escape hatch was closing to her now. She could build up no resentment for Michael.

And the very idea of it seemed terrifyingly dangerous.

"You should get some rest," he said abruptly.

"I'm not tired." She straightened away from the doorjamb. "But you must be. I can take the wheel for a while."

"You aren't familiar enough with these waters."

"You have the course marked out, and I can read the instruments. Let me take over for a few hours at least, Michael. If you don't get some rest, you aren't going to be able to think straight. And that's an edge we're going to need."

He couldn't argue, because she was right. He was so tired he was barely thinking straight now—and the sun promised to bring a very long day.

"All right." He stepped back to allow her to take the wheel, managing somehow not to touch her. "Can you handle it until five?"

"Hardly enough time for you to get a decent rest. I can—"

"Five, Robin. By then we'll be too close to the island to take any chances. At five shut down the engine and let her drift. Wake me then." He knew the engine shutdown would wake him in any event.

"All right," she agreed reluctantly.

Dane Prescott looked up from the poker hands he was absently dealing on the coffee table, and grimaced slightly. "You could have used the front door," he said dryly. "I hear the lock's easy as hell to pick."

His visitor stepped away from the open French doors leading out onto the balcony. Coming fully into the room, he crossed to the group of sofas and made himself comfortable across from Dane. "I needed the exercise," he said calmly.

"We're sixteen floors up. Don't tell me you climbed?"

"No. Down from the roof. You just dealt a ten into a low flush. You're slipping."

Ignoring the observation, Dane gathered up the cards and lifted a brow questioningly at his visitor. "You were supposed to be up north somewhere."

"Best-laid plans, and all that. You had another visitor tonight."

With some feeling Dane said, "I've been having visitors all day. You'd think a man could run a decent con without agents coming out of the woodwork."

The visitor smiled slightly. "At least none of us are after you this time."

"Agents are never after me, Skye. Police sometimes, but never agents."

"Raven Long," Skye prompted.

Dane closed his eyes briefly. "I knew you were going to say that."

At five A.M., with dawn barely showing in the eastern sky, Robin shut the engine off and released the wheel, absently flexing her stiff hands. The abrupt silence was unsettling, with only the soft slapping of the waves against the boat breaking the predawn quiet. She stood for a few moments, adjusting to the altered motion of the boat, then sighed and left the cramped bridge.

The air was misty and held a faint chill, the darkness shading toward gray, and Robin felt very alone. She could see no sign of land or another boat. According to the course Michael had marked out, their position was between three and five miles from the outermost of the Ten Thousand Islands and their approach from the southwest.

Robin stood on deck for a few minutes, then slowly made her way below. A light flicked on just as she entered the cabin, and she found Michael sitting on the bunk and looking completely alert.

"It's a quarter after five," she offered. "According to your charts, we should be a few miles from the islands." Before he could respond, she added lightly, "Is that galley stove as complicated as it looks? If not, I thought I'd have a shot at fixing breakfast."

Michael had slept in his jeans, and now rose to pull his T-shirt over his head. "It isn't complicated," he said in a close match of her tone. "The fuel's gas; ignition's automatic. Just turn the dials."

She thought the shadow of his beard made him look like a pirate. She told herself to stop thinking like that. "I should be able to handle it, then. Any preferences?"

"No. But you should get some sleep, Robin."

"I will. When I want it." She turned away and took two steps down the short hall to the extremely compact galley. There was barely room to move in there, and she found the light switch easily enough. The first thing she did was put water on for coffee.

As Michael started to move past the galley, she asked, "Will we be getting under way again soon? I'm not so sure I can cook in here if we're moving." She didn't look at him.

"We'll drift for a while. I want to take closer look at the charts before we head toward the islands."

Robin nodded and concentrated on finding out where everything was stored in the tiny kitchen. Tried to concentrate, anyway, but she was all too aware of his soft footsteps moving away. She didn't want to think anymore. The hours she had spent at the wheel had been some of the longest of her life, and had allowed far too much time for thought.

She had reminded herself over and over that the attraction between her and Michael was just that—an attraction. And simply because B followed A, it didn't inevitably follow that an attraction between two people had to be acted on. It was the wrong time, the wrong place—and each of them had too many demons chasing them.

She told herself those things over and over. Futilely. Offering to prepare breakfast had not been sparked by the drive of hunger but rather by the need to be busy, to *do* something. Unfortunately she was too good a cook to have to pay attention to what she was doing; and her mind wouldn't be distracted from dwelling on disturbing things.

Her emotions were jumbled, her self-knowledge was askew for the first time in years, and she was powerfully drawn to a man she hardly understood. A man who didn't bet on long shots. Danger lay behind her, and ahead of her, and there were lives at stake.

Normal is what you get accustomed to.

Her own words, spoken to reassure Michael that his sister's life had most likely been, to her, normal. But Robin knew Michael's life wasn't "normal." A man would never become accustomed to dangers that threatened the emotions and the spirit as well as the body. And especially not if that man gave hostages to fortune in the shape of a sister . . . or a lover.

At the same time Robin also knew this *was* Michael's life, by his own choice, and not likely to change. Men like Michael wouldn't change course often, or easily. If he lived long enough, he would doubtless one day head an agency, like her father, where the field work would be limited. Limited—but not nonexistent. His would always be a dangerous life.

Realizing her thoughts were becoming entirely too wrapped up in speculation on the future, Robin hastily forced herself to concentrate on the cooking. But it was hard.

She called Michael when the meal was ready, and they ate sitting across from each other at a tiny booth that took up half the galley space. Robin was silent, highly conscious that her chaotic emotions could easily present a danger in the coming hours; Michael was equally quiet and preoccupied.

She didn't speak until he rose to carry his plate to the tiny sink and rinse it. The automatic action caused her a curious pang, and she thought, *He's been alone a long time.*

"Michael?"

He was refilling his coffee cup and leaned back against the doorjamb instead of returning to the booth. "Yeah?" he responded quietly.

"When all this is over, and Lisa's safe again, what will you do?" She wasn't about to suggest a different ending to the tragic situation—and she couldn't stop thinking of the future.

He looked at her steadily. "If you're asking whether I'll decide to get into another line of work because of what's happened to Lisa, the answer is no. I would if Lisa asked me to, but she won't." He hesitated, then said roughly, "I don't know anything else, Robin. This is the life I was trained for, the life I know better than any other. I wasn't naive when I made my choice years ago, I knew what it meant. I don't regret my choice."

She had been right, but it didn't make it easier. "I see. I thought that was the way you felt."

"And so?" It sounded like a reluctant question, as if he weren't sure he wanted an answer.

"And so . . I'm not surprised by your answer. You wouldn't be in this business if the answer had been different."

"Then why did you ask?" Another reluctant question.

Robin looked at him and forced a wry smile. "Just trying to find out what really makes a hero tick, I guess."

"Study somebody else, then. I'm no hero."

She returned her gaze to her coffee, unable to hold her own with his restless but intent eyes. She could feel something happening inside her, as if a door had opened, allowing her to see something in herself she'd never before seen. Hardly aware of speaking, she murmured, "Maybe that's the charm of real heroes; they don't know they *are*."

Michael set his cup aside and took one step to reach the booth, grasping her arms and pulling her abruptly to her feet. "Get it through your head," he said tightly. "There's not one damn thing that's heroic about me, Robin. I do the job I'm paid to do because I happen to be good at it. If I were good with plants, I'd be a gardener, good with engines I'd be a mechanic."

She stared up at him, trying desperately to resent the strength in him, the purpose. She couldn't. "But you happen to be good at doing dangerous things. And you almost never bet on long shots."

A muscle tightened in his jaw. "Never. Not this kind."

"What if the long shot bets on you?"

"It's one chance in a million, Robin, and more than odds against us. You'd only get hurt."

Robin didn't move as he turned away, and spoke only when he was at the door. "What about you?" she asked unsteadily.

He paused for an instant to look back at her, his face taut and eyes burning. "Me too," he muttered, and headed topside.

After a while she moved automatically to clean up the galley. She felt shaken by what she had seen in herself—and by what she had seen in Michael. In both cases there was pressure building, something growing beyond their abilities to control it. And they both knew it. Neither could run, and there wasn't time enough to just stop and try to think it through. It was like watching a storm overtaking you, Robin thought, and knowing you were powerless to stop it or escape it.

Storms often left a shambles in their wake; she didn't know what this would leave.

Robin wanted to stay below and try to pull herself together, but the sound of the engine of an approaching boat impelled her to quickly climb to the deck. And she almost welcomed the diversion, even though her common sense told her it could mean trouble. But she had barely reached the deck when the hail from an approaching cabin cruiser stopped her in astonishment.

"Ahoy!"

"It's Teddy," she said blankly as Michael reached her side. She barely had time to notice he held a gun in one hand before he'd slipped it inside the waistband of his jeans at the small of his back. "How in the world . . . ?"

"Looks like we'll get the chance to ask," Michael answered dryly, studying the boat as it slowed, and finally drifted to come alongside with a gentle bump.

Teddy, her riotous mass of red hair flaming around her small, vivid face, leaned over the side of the bigger cruiser and grinned down at them. "Hi, there."

"What're you *doing* here?" Robin asked.

"We're the cavalry, of course," Teddy responded, unperturbed. As two other women joined her, she introduced them. "This is Raven Long, and our skipper here is Kyle Kendrick." She directed her interested gaze to Michael. "I'm Teddy Steele. And you must be the captain."

"Michael," he said, and nodded slightly at Raven, the only one of the three he had met before. "Mrs. Long."

"Raven," she corrected him, then gestured to the boats. "Can we lash these two beasts together? We need a conference."

Five minutes later Michael and Robin had joined the women on their boat, which was considerably larger than his. And Michael, highly conscious of passing time, didn't waste any of it.

"I don't know how much you know," he said, "but I'm on a tight schedule and—"

"The *Dragon Lady*," Raven interrupted calmly, "is anchored at the Maze. It's all right; Dane's keeping an eye on it."

"Dane?"

"Surprised me too," she said, smiling a little as she leaned back in her deck chair. "I saw him late last night and got the story out of him. We were about to leave Miami a couple of hours later when he showed up and said he was coming along."

Michael frowned, a bit unsettled. "Just don't tell me he's watching the yacht in plain sight and wearing one of his famous white suits."

"You wouldn't know him," Raven assured him. "He's in a little fishing boat, decked out with everything from a fly-covered hat to a bottle in a brown bag. Occasionally he bursts into drunken song or creative swearing. There are, by the way, half a dozen other such fishermen in that area, all perfectly legitimate; you couldn't pick Dane out of the bunch."

Still frowning, Michael said, "I still don't like it. If there's that much activity in the area, Sutton has to be getting nervous."

"Doubtful," Kyle told him. "There happens to be a fishing tournament going on, and it's an annual thing. Some of the men on Sutton's yacht have dropped lines into the water; looks like they're using the event as cover themselves."

Michael relaxed somewhat. "And what about you ladies?"

Teddy grinned at him. "We've been zipping in and out of the islands getting yelled at for disturbing the fish. Raven said that the best way to get into a situation where you couldn't help drawing attention to yourself was to draw a *lot* of attention."

Eyeing the three women dressed in bright swim-suits that would have turned the head of a stone statue, Michael had no trouble believing they'd drawn a great deal of attention. "I see."

"We know the whole story," Raven told him, seri-ous now. "We're here to help, Michael."

"Look, I appreciate what you're trying to do." He had no difficulty in sounding sincere. "But Sutton has a hair-trigger finger, and his men are worse. You can't— "

"*You* can't do it alone," Raven told him. "Two against at least a dozen? No matter how good you are, you can't ignore the odds. And Sutton doesn't know any of us; you're the red flag."

"It's too dangerous. I can't ask—"

"You're not asking," Teddy said, studying her fin-gernails with a frown.

Michael drew a deep breath and, without looking at Robin, said tautly, "You came to help Robin. Help the both of us by getting her out of this mess now, before she gets hurt."

"I'd say it was too late for that," Kyle said quietly.

Michael glanced at Robin and wished he hadn't; the hurt in her eyes was obvious. He felt like a bastard.

Raven leaned forward and held his gaze with vio-let eyes that had suddenly gone dark and hard. "You may not know much about our abilities, *Captain*, but you do know Hagen has pulled us into messes like this for the past few years. What we didn't know in the beginning, we've learned. And if that doesn't convince you, I'll tell you something else. I know exactly what those girls on the yacht are going through. *Exactly*. Because I've been there myself.

Because my sister died at the hands of slavers. I could no more walk away from this 'mess' than I could stop breathing—and that goes for my friends here."

After a long moment Michael said, "I'm sorry. Ever since I found out Sutton had Lisa, all I've been able to think about is how responsible I am for it." He sighed roughly. "But you're right. All those girls have to be gotten off the yacht safely. And I can't do it alone." He looked at Robin, adding, "I'm sorry, Robin."

She didn't return his gaze, but nodded slightly.

Raven glanced at them curiously for a moment, then sat back in her chair. "We didn't exactly come up with a plan," she told Michael, "but we have started a couple of things in motion."

"What things?"

Teddy answered. "Sutton will leave the yacht about midafternoon today. And it's a good bet he'll take at least a couple of his men when he goes."

"Goes?" Michael looked at them. "Goes where?"

"He'll have to take care of a business crisis," Raven said limpidly.

"How did you manage that?" Michael asked blankly.

"It wasn't too difficult. Dane found out that Sutton has a hell of a lot invested in various gambling parlors in Miami. It was fairly simple to gather all the addresses together and arrange to tip the police."

"It could be days before he'd find out," Michael objected slowly.

But Raven was shaking her head. "This time he's going to hear about it by afternoon. Dane said you'd remember the man with the diamonds." She waited for Michael's nod, then continued. "It seems that man is a close friend of Sutton's, and a business partner. Not public knowledge, you understand. Dane had a game scheduled with him for tonight in one of Sutton's places. Dane also has a trusted friend who's going to get a message to Mr. Diamonds by lunchtime warning him that Dane's heard all those parlors are going to be raided tonight. Mr. Diamonds, by the way, is in the habit of looking to Sutton for guidance, and he knows Sutton is aboard the *Dragon Lady*. He also knows where the yacht anchors, and Sutton's emergency radio frequency."

Michael was impressed. In fact, he was delighted. "How on earth did you manage so much in just a few hours? And how, by the way, did you arrive here before us?"

Kyle smiled at him. "We've been taught a number of devious tricks. We also have—between us—contacts all over the country. We got all the information on Sutton before we left New York, thanks to Robin's very complete package to Teddy. Dane did most of the rest."

"As for how we got here so quickly," Teddy said, "it was in a helicopter from Miami. A jet helicopter. And we've rented a big house on the coast no more than a mile from the Maze. This cruiser came with the house."

Michael mulled that over for a moment, and it was Robin who asked the next question.

"You said you'd set a couple of things in motion. What's the other thing?"

Calmly Raven said, "The news will break sometime *after* Sutton leaves the yacht that the fishing tournament in the area has a special prize this year. It will be announced by the local radio station—which Sutton's men listen to constantly."

"What prize?" Michael asked.

"Twenty thousand dollars to the fisherman who brings in the biggest catch," Raven said. "Within an hour the entire area should be bow to stern with hopeful anglers."

"Damn." Michael looked at her thoughtfully. "And since Sutton's men will know about it, and won't be able to wave their guns around to ward off the crowd—"

"A plausible diversion," Robin said softly. "They'll be paying so much attention to the fishermen, they won't even notice us."

"We should be able to get close," Raven agreed.

"Have you already arranged that?" Michael asked.

"Pending your approval," Teddy told him. "The contest officials and the radio station will be notified as soon as Sutton leaves the yacht. And the prize is being offered—officially—by a company in the area that handles fishing equipment. If any of Sutton's men are suspicious enough to call and check it out, they'll find the deal's legitimate all the way."

"And just to make sure we don't find ourselves tripping over eager fishermen," Raven said wryly, "Dane was busy before the sun rose, casually passing the word among his fellow fisherman that the best fishing is around the two islands south of the Maze. Those islands are close but not too close. So, hopefully, while Sutton's men are watching the water traffic to their south, we can circle around, cross the island from the north, and reach the yacht while their attention's focused elsewhere."

Michael looked at them for a moment, a smile tugging at his lips. "Is there a base you haven't covered?"

"That was the easy stuff," Teddy dismissed. "The trick is still going to be getting the girls off the yacht. Distracted or not, those men are armed. Six of us, counting Dane, but we can't just swarm over the boat."

"When the cat's away . . ." Robin murmured suddenly in a thoughtful tone.

Raven met her eyes, then nodded slowly. "Maybe. If we could lead a few of those guys astray, get them off the yacht . . ."

"They're professionals," Michael objected, seeing where this was leading and not happy about it.

"And they've been under a great deal of strain," Raven pointed out. "Stuck on that boat and not allowed to touch the girls. The girls are probably drugged; certainly they're locked in a cabin or two. They don't really *need* all those guards. And maybe a few of those guys would love to be invited to a party."

Michael narrowed his eyes. "If we survive this, your husbands will lynch me."

"They'd be the first to understand," Teddy assured him blithely.

"What if the guards bring their guns to the party?" Robin asked.

Raven smiled slightly. "Teddy brought her usual supply of tranquilizer darts; we'll be armed too."

"I don't like it," Michael said.

Robin looked at him levelly. "What choice do we have?"

He nodded slowly, getting the point. "You're right. What choice do we have?"

Five

The *Black Angel* rode her sea anchor easily on the calm water, engines silent. Michael hadn't dared take her in any closer, wary of risking Sutton's recognition of the boat. Nor was he prepared to circle around to the north, leaving his enemy with a clear escape route to the south. He and the women agreed that if Sutton moved at all, he would most likely head south since that presented his best chances of leaving U.S. territory quickly and safely.

All of them knew they were battling the clock. Their best guess was that Sutton had initially planned to have only Lisa on his yacht by the time Michael came hunting him; the crackdown on boats around the coast had forced him to keep the other girls aboard days longer than was safe or practical. He would soon be forced to decide which was his priority: revenge against Michael or the valuable cargo of the girls.

Both Michael and Dane felt strongly that revenge

would come out on top; therefore, they had to move against Sutton before he decided to cut his losses. He was a man who took few chances, and the girls would never be freed alive.

Michael knew only too well that the plan he'd agreed to with the others was one that depended on a number of opinions and instincts. And the linchpin of their entire plan was that Sutton would return to Miami once he heard of the danger to his investments. Only then could they hope to lessen the odds against them by attempting to "divide and conquer" the security force on the yacht.

And since both Michael and Robin were the "red flag" and too likely to be recognized by either Sutton or his crew, they were more or less forced to remain several miles from the islands—and wait.

"What about Sutton?" Robin asked suddenly. They were both on deck, shaded from the ten o'clock sun by an awning, and neither was handling the waiting very well.

Michael didn't need the question clarified. Gazing off toward the islands with restless eyes, he said, "If Sutton isn't on the yacht physically, there isn't much chance of building a case against him in court. We couldn't prove ownership of the yacht, and unless the girls identify him as being in charge . . ."

"Do you think they will?"

"I don't think Sutton's given them the chance to see him."

"What about Lisa?"

"Maybe. But I doubt it. He's too cautious for that."

"Then he'll get away with it?" Robin regretted the question the instant she saw Michael's jaw tighten.

"No."

In the steadiest voice she could manage, she said, "You'll go after him yourself. Once Lisa and the others are safe?"

"One way or another," Michael said softly, "Sutton's going to pay for what he's done."

Shying away from what that might mean, Robin changed the subject. "You were very surprised Dane involved himself. Raven seemed to be as well."

Michael shrugged slightly. "From what I know of him—and what Raven obviously knows—it's a bit out of character. I've seen him turn in performances worthy of awards, but he tends to avoid other people's problems."

"He's certainly not avoiding this problem. Maybe he's more of a friend than you thought."

"Or maybe he has his own reasons."

Robin felt a pang. "You don't trust easily."

He was silent.

"Do you trust me?" she asked.

After a long moment he said roughly, "Yes."

"Why does that disturb you so much? That you trust me? Because trust leaves you vulnerable?"

"I don't think we want to get into this," Michael said.

It had been a mistake, Robin realized, for her to have remained with him. Teddy had suggested that she might want to head back toward the Maze with them, remaining in the cabin of the larger cruiser. But Robin had refused with a slight shake of her head, and Michael had said nothing.

She should have gone with them. The tension of waiting, added to the tension already present between her and Michael, left them both with precarious control. And they were too alone, too conscious of each other. That he had the self-awareness to warn her off from unstable emotional ground was remarkable; Robin felt herself lacking in that awareness at the moment.

"I always did have lousy timing," she murmured at last.

Michael stirred slightly, but still didn't turn and look at her. "Robin . . ."

"No, it's all right. The waiting's getting to me, I guess. And when I'm nervous, I ask questions. Sorry."

Michael was trying. He was trying to ignore the building desire he felt for her, trying to fight the tangle of emotions that everything inside him mistrusted. But he had to warn her, had to make her understand. She hadn't been in a situation like this, and couldn't know how easy it was to allow the circumstances to dictate far too much.

He turned his head finally, looking at her. "I've seen it happen before," he said.

"What?" She wasn't sure she wanted to know.

"Situations like this." His voice sounded curiously suspended, caught somewhere between control and chaos. "So many negative elements. Tension. Danger. Anxiety. Events that are impossible to control or influence. Time . . . dragging one minute and racing the next. Living on a knife-edge. And that's a hell of a place to—"

"To what?"

Sitting two feet away from her, expressionless, Michael answered quietly, "To fall in love."

For a moment Robin couldn't breathe. And her own voice was low and rushed. "That isn't it."

"No?"

"No." She tried to steady her voice, tried to deny

what he had seen, what he had guessed. "It's just chemistry, and everything that's happened makes it feel—seem—stronger than it really is. But—"

He interrupted her, his voice still quiet. "As I said, I've seen it happen. Again and again, against all reason. Two people thrown together in a situation boiling with negative emotions, the worst possible foundation for love. No time to stop to think, just a compulsion."

"It isn't real," she whispered.

"It's always real, Robin. But it rarely lasts."

She realized, then, what he was telling her. "And that's the long shot you won't bet on."

He glanced off toward the distant islands for a moment, then looked back at her. "We'll all come out of this with scars, Robin. You, me, Lisa, those other girls—even your friends and Dane. We'll all be different, marked somewhere inside. Situations like this always mark you. It may not show on the surface, but each of us will know it's true. And it doesn't matter whether we win or lose. We'll all be *changed.*"

He drew a deep breath, released it slowly. "And believing that love born in turmoil will last . . . is inviting another kind of scar. The kind of scar that probably wouldn't ever heal."

Robin, realizing, said, "It's happened to you before."

"Yes," he said flatly.

He wasn't ready to talk about it, she realized. If he ever would be. It was Robin's turn to draw a steadying breath. "Part of me understands what you're saying. But part of me doesn't. I don't hedge bets."

"Don't you?" Michael smiled just a little, adding gently, "You hedged the biggest bet of your life."

"No." She didn't want to hear what he was about to say, but there was nowhere to run.

"Becoming a cop, Robin. You didn't trust yourself, didn't trust your ability to control your fear. And you failed the exam."

"I tried," she said tightly. "I did my best."

"Be honest with yourself. If you had failed because you really didn't want to be a cop, you wouldn't be involved in this situation now."

Robin looked away, unable to meet his steady gaze. "Neat change of subject," she said, admitting nothing.

"I don't think so. How many times in the past have you become attracted to some kind of cop?"

She felt her throat tighten, tension build. "So that's where you're going with this," she said. "You're saying this between us is even more unreal because I'm in the habit of falling for cops. Do you specialize in armchair analysis?"

"I specialize in survival," he said softly.

She knew that was true; despite the present situation, Michael was indeed a survivor. He wouldn't have lasted past his first assignment in this business otherwise. And even though she *did* understand why he was refusing to give in to the needs and emotions between them, it hurt too much for her to be able to ignore the pain and accept his rational doubts.

He had been right about her past involvement with cops, but she knew with a certainty she'd never felt before that these feelings were different. Without the illusion of a "superman," a nerveless, fearless superior being standing between them, she had no doubts about her own feelings. And though his mistrust of the longevity of fragile emotions in a dangerous situation was all too reasonable, she really thought he was wrong about their chances. It was the wrong time and the wrong place, but the feelings were real.

Real—and he was going to ignore them.

If she let him.

She looked up to find him gone, and after a moment rose and went below. The door to the tiny bathroom was closed, and she heard the shower running inside. So. He thought the discussion was over, an agreement reached. He believed she was as wary of hurts that left scars as he was himself.

And aren't I?

It didn't seem to matter. A compulsion, he said? Was that what she was feeling? Her fingers moved of their own volition, unfastening buttons; she shrugged off her blouse, nudged off the shoes, and slid the cutoff jeans down her legs.

They had hours, at least. Maybe at most. And she refused to allow a fear of scars to stop her. This time she intended to master at least one fear.

The cramped bathroom was filled with steam, and Robin didn't know whether to laugh or cry when she remembered just how tiny the shower stall was. But she had gone too far to let logistics determine her course from here. Taking a deep breath, she pulled aside the curtain and slipped into the stall.

Michael turned immediately, so close that his arm brushed her breast and made both of them inhale sharply. His eyes cut through the fog of steam, sweeping down her naked body.

"Robin, get out of here," he said huskily.

She shook her head slowly, and deliberately stepped closer, her hands lifting to rest on his broad chest.

The dark, wet hair covering his muscled flesh was a tactile delight, and her fingers stroked it compulsively. She hadn't realized he would be so beautiful, but he was, and the sight of him moved her more than she would have believed possible. "I can't do that," she said.

He reached behind him to turn off the water, and the sudden silence was stark. "Robin—"

She rose on tiptoe, her arms sliding up around his neck, her body molding itself to his. And she could feel his instant response, feel the taut hardening of his body. His eyes were darkening, and a muscle leapt in his jaw. As if he couldn't help himself, his arms went around her damp body.

"Damn you," he whispered just before his lips covered hers.

As before, Robin felt the instant surge of heat, the wildfire running through her veins. Her heart had swelled in her breast, thudding frantically, and there was no strength in her legs. She felt his hands slide down to cup her buttocks, pulling her even more firmly against him, and sounds she didn't recognize tangled in the back of her throat.

He was taking her mouth, she realized dimly, possessing it, demanding it with a force she had never encountered before meeting him. But something in her answered that force once again, rising to meet it, surging up from deep inside her. It seemed almost a battle, a clash of wills, and she didn't know what they were fighting against.

Or fighting for.

When he tore his lips from hers suddenly, Robin almost cried out in disappointment. But then Michael swept the shower curtain aside and guided her out of the cramped bathroom and to the cabin. Immediately he pulled her back into his arms. His eyes glittered, and there was a bittersweet curve to his lips.

"You don't know what you've done," he said roughly.

Robin thought she was lost somewhere in his eyes, and the words escaped before she could stop them. "You were right. I love you, Michael."

"You won't tomorrow," he said.

She had no way of convincing him. And so much could happen by tomorrow. "Make love to me," she whispered.

Michael half closed his eyes, but even then he was lifting her, placing her on the bunk, joining her there. "I knew that first night that you were dangerous," he said, the words a rough caress as his lips explored her soft throat. "You held on to me so tightly when I pulled you from the water, and I didn't like the way it made me feel."

She threaded her fingers through the heavy weight of his wet hair, hearing his voice and feeling the throbbing surge of heat all through her. "How did it make you feel?"

"Caught." He laughed tautly. "Caught by something I'd never be able to let go. Oh, Robin . . ." His lips trailed down over her breastbone, then feathered hotly over a swelling mound until he captured her nipple.

Robin gasped, half arching against him. She had never believed such feelings were possible, and knew now that she was willing to pay any price for this. She could barely breathe, and the erotic touch of his mouth was driving her mad. Desperate to touch him, she probed the shifting muscles of his back and shoulders, her fingers learning him. She felt strength and power, and the heat of his damp flesh burned her.

Michael wanted to lose himself in her, to allow passion to carry them both to a place where no danger lurked, where no clock ticked away the remorseless passing of minutes. She was in his bloodstream, underneath his skin, and the only remedy for the maddening ache was this. He knew he would pay a price, and even knowing the cost would be his heart held no power to stop him. It was too late for that.

He couldn't get enough of her. The softness of her skin drew him, the heat of her fed his own fire, and her instant, total response compelled him. The touch of her hands was velvet, was exquisite torture. His heart was pounding out of control in his chest, his breathing ragged.

Her belly quivered as his hand slid slowly down, and she moaned when he eased her legs apart. His touch was gentle but insistent, fingers probing until he found the slick heat. Robin was hardly aware of her nails digging into his back; all her senses were caught up in the exquisite pleasure he was teaching her body to feel so wildly.

On some level of her consciousness Robin realized that Michael was a silent lover. And on that same level of herself, she saw and understood that he was holding back, that he was, even in this jarring intimacy, guarding himself. Shut inside himself for so long, he couldn't abandon his defenses even here, even now.

It made her own need stronger, her own abandonment more complete. She took fire entirely, burning, offering everything she was to him and demanding everything he would give to her. And what he wouldn't give she tried to steal.

He took her right to the brink before he finally moved over her, settling between her thighs, and Robin thought she might not be able to survive the spiraling tension inside her. She felt the blunt pressure against her aching flesh, felt the hard length of him sinking into her body, and the slight pain brought only a quick gasp.

Then there was nothing but rising pleasure, until she wasn't aware of anything else, until her body was a single throbbing, aching need. Her limbs held him with all the strength she could command, even as her body held him, until the pleasure exploded in a release so devastating she felt she'd shattered inside.

She was barely aware of Michael's rasping groan, and when his heavy weight settled fully on her, she held him tightly.

It wasn't until his pulse had slowed to something near normal that Michael found the strength to raise his head and ease some of his weight onto his arms. She was looking up at him with those heartbreaking green eyes, and he bent his head to kiss her because he had to. Her response was immediate, and total. He wondered vaguely if he had any control left to him.

"You should have told me," he said finally when he lifted his head.

With an odd little smile she said softly, "Then you *really* would have fought me."

He wanted to shake her. He wanted to kiss her again, make love to her again. "Dammit, Robin."

"Hey, I'm over twenty-one," she told him dryly.

He kissed the smiling mouth again, unable to resist. "Your age has nothing to do with it," he said, managing to hold his voice steady and even. "You'll be hurt by this, Robin. You haven't settled with your own demons yet, and now you're ready to take on mine?"

Her smile faded, and the green eyes went grave. "I do have a few kicking around in the dark, don't I?"

"Yes, you do."

"Then help me fight them."

Michael found himself tracing her delicate features with one finger, conscious of an absurd sense of wonder that her skin could be so soft. "Honey, I can't even fight my own."

"I do love you, you know," she said.

He felt something inside him clench in pain. "Today."

"And tomorrow." Her voice was steady. "And next week. Shall I go on?"

"You don't know me," he said through the tightness in his throat.

"Michael, I know all I'll ever need to know about you."

"And what about my life?" He cleared his throat roughly. "I'm the one with the dirty gray hat, remember? That isn't going to change. Home is this boat more often than not. I'm not cut out for a desk and a mortgage, Robin."

"What makes you think I am?" Before he could answer, she added quietly, "I'm not making demands, if that's what you think. But I love you, and I wanted you to know."

"All right." He could feel the growing tension in her, and he didn't want to talk about it any longer. Their time together could well be brief hours, and he didn't want to waste any of it. "All right, honey. We'll talk about it later."

Michael could feel the renewal of desire, and if his inner self reminded him of just how brief time could be, if his experienced inner voice nudged him with the knowledge that "later" sometimes never came, he chose to ignore it. He lowered his head and kissed her, conscious of her instant response and trying to keep the sharp edge of desperation out of his own.

At two o'clock that afternoon the big cabin cruiser containing Raven, Kyle, and Teddy narrowly avoided running down a small launch as it left the island called the Maze and headed toward the coast.

"Sorry!" Raven sang out, waving from her position at the wheel and hearing curses from the skipper of the launch. She aimed the cruiser to circle around the island, her nonchalant glance toward the half-hidden cove taking in a great deal.

Kyle appeared suddenly beside her. "If Luc comes back soon," she said, "I'm going to have to explain this bruise."

"What bruise?" Raven asked.

"The one I got when your last maneuver slammed me against the table in the galley. I love you, Raven, but putting you at the wheel of a boat is more than my nerves can stand. May I take over now?"

"Certainly." Unoffended, Raven stepped aside. She

grinned faintly. "I thought the rest of you had learned by now that I can just barely be trusted with a car, much less any other moving vehicle."

The erratic motion of the big boat had settled the instant Kyle took over, and she laughed softly. "Well, Teddy can't steer, so I had to take a chance on you. A lesson well learned."

Raven reached for the radio near the wheel and made a brief call, then cradled the handset.

"Was that Sutton rushing by a few minutes ago?" Teddy asked, joining them and absently rubbing her hip.

"In the flesh. With at least three of his men." Raven looked at the broad masculine watch on her wrist. "And right on time too. I bet he has a helicopter coming to pick him up. We'll wait just long enough to make sure he doesn't send his men back to the yacht."

"Then we call the captain and Robin?"

Raven nodded.

Thoughtfully Kyle said, "An interesting man, the captain. Doesn't give much away, does he?"

"Not much, no," Raven agreed dryly.

Kyle smiled, remembering when Raven's ex-partner, Kelsey, had directed that same accusation at herself. "People with that kind of control," she noted neutrally, "generally spend years earning it. Do you think he's as dangerous as he looks?"

"I'd say he's more dangerous than he looks," Raven said. "Kelsey told me what he knew, and the upshot is that Captain Michael Siran is a deadly enemy . . . and a wary friend."

Teddy winced. "That doesn't sound good for Robin.

Or was I the only one who noticed how she looked at him?"

"You weren't," Kyle said. "Although I got the feeling that Michael is far from indifferent."

"You're perspective," Raven told her with a faint smile. "He hardly let it show at all."

Teddy continued to worry. "Oh, damn, is he another Zach? That nearly killed me."

Raven leaned back against an instrument panel, her gaze turning absently to study the Maze as they cruised around it. "The situation's a bit different," she said, referring to the battle Teddy had gone through to convince her own lone-wolf warrior that she belonged at his side. "Robin knows cops if she knows anything at all, and from what Kelsey told me, Michael walks alone more by habit than choice."

"She can take care of herself," Teddy offered hopefully. "I've never seen anyone better at it than Robin."

"Mmm." Raven sighed. "We'll have to wait and see. Things are moving awfully fast, and there's rough water ahead. If they make it through—well, who knows?"

"I'll cross my fingers," Teddy said, sighing as well.

Raven smiled at her, then looked at their skipper. "Kyle, on our next pass, stop by Dane's boat."

"Right," Kyle answered.

"Now, *he* definitely bothers me," Teddy offered, frowning a little. "Raven, didn't you call him an information broker? That's hardly the part he's playing now."

Raven shrugged. "I guess he wears two hats. We certainly can't complain so far."

"Yes, but how will he be when the pressure's really on? I mean, the way we've set this up, he and Michael will be the ones going aboard Sutton's yacht. Even if we manage to draw some of the guards away, that still leaves several on the yacht."

Raven smiled a little. "Don't worry about Dane. I've seen him in a few tough spots. He can handle himself."

Teddy nodded, accepting Raven's judgment. "Has the radio station made the announcement yet?"

"Should be any time now," Raven answered. "I called our guy at the fishing equipment company, and he's on his way."

"Lucky that Long Enterprises is into fishing gear," Kyle said.

"I wonder why," Raven said musingly. "Josh doesn't even like to fish."

"Here we go," Kyle said, cutting back on the speed as they neared the island closest to the Maze.

Teddy and Raven both headed for the deck, and both enjoyed the sight of Dane sitting alone in his small boat with fishing paraphernalia piled all around him.

He was playing his part to the hilt, as Raven had told Michael, completely with a fly-covered hat and a bottle in a brown bag. Anyone getting close enough might have noticed that the bottle contained fruit juice, but it certainly seemed like a pint of whiskey. Dane hadn't shaved in preparation for his role, and the blue shadowing partially hid the classic bone structure that made his jaw rather memorable. With his hat pulled low, rumpled clothing, and the bottle, he certainly passed muster as a fisherman out for a rousing good time.

He bellowed out a ribald greeting as the big cruiser floated near, but the instant the engines were cut, his voice dropped to its normal deep and almost melodic tones.

"Tell me why people actually do this for recreation?" he requested of Raven in a pained voice.

She leaned over the side and grinned down at him. "Beats me. I've always considered it a rather unequal contest. Unless, of course, you catch something bigger than you are."

He glanced around with mock uneasiness. "Don't say that. I saw a shark movie years ago and haven't put a toe in the ocean since."

"I saw the same movie. But we've got more to worry about today than killer sharks."

"Agreed." He took a drink from his disguised juice bottle, and looked steadily at her, his expression serious now. "I saw Sutton and company go roaring by. When do we move?"

"We'll wait about an hour to make sure he doesn't send his men back to the yacht, and to give him time to get well on his way to Miami. Then we'll call Michael and Robin and have them start moving this way."

Dane glanced at his watch, a complicated-looking sportsman's watch that was far different from what he usually wore. "A little after two now. That means we'll probably all be in position by four."

Raven nodded. "Michael's boat will circle around to the little inlet on the other side of the Maze, and meet you there. Robin will stay with the boat—"

"Will she?" Dane interrupted.

Raven and Teddy exchanged glances, and Raven looked back at him intently. "What's on your mind?"

"Call it a hunch." Dane frowned a little. "I got the feeling the lady has a lot to prove to herself."

"She wouldn't endanger Michael's sister and the other girls," Teddy objected.

"No, I agree with you there. But she won't like Michael boarding a yacht full of guards either." He shrugged. "Like I said, it's just a hunch."

Raven nodded. "And it's Michael's call. We've taken care of all the details we could; the rest'll be luck and timing."

"Speaking of which"—Dane looked at them steadily—"sure you ladies want to entice those guards off the yacht? That's a dangerous game."

"We can handle it," Teddy told him cheerfully. "Once we get them below, they won't know what hit them."

He nodded, not so much doubtful as uneasy. "If you say so. Watch yourselves, though. I don't relish the idea of having to explain to your husbands if something goes wrong."

"Our husbands," Raven told him lightly, "would be the first to understand."

As they straightened away from the side, Dane prepared to return to his fishing. But they both heard his muttered comment before Kyle started the engines again.

"Sure," he told his fishing rod dryly.

Robin hadn't intended to cling to Michael as he headed the boat toward their target island, but he took the decision out of her hands. Once they were under way, he simply pulled her against his side and held her there, keeping one hand on the wheel.

She wasn't reluctant, and slipped both arms around

his lean waist. "Thanks," she said unsteadily. "I was feeling a little shaky."

"So am I," he said, kissing her forehead gently.

"It'll be all right," she told him fiercely, rubbing her cheek against his chest. "Lisa and the other girls will be fine."

"I know."

Robin braced herself inwardly. "When you and Dane slip aboard the yacht, I—I'm going with you."

Michael had been expecting that. He could have argued all the drawbacks, and argued convincingly. Robin was inexperienced at this kind of situation. She strongly mistrusted her own abilities and was convinced her fear would paralyze her. Still, he knew, she had unresolved feelings of guilt over having escaped when the other girls hadn't, and she was furiously angry at the men responsible.

In a very real sense she was a ticking bomb that would either be safely defused . . . or blow up.

And that was why Michael couldn't ignore her determination. If he refused to allow her to come with him and Dane for the sake of her own safety, her feelings of inadequacy would prompt her to hear the words: *I don't have any faith in you either. I think you'll freeze.*

He couldn't do such a thing to her. Even though the stakes were agonizingly high, the simple fact was he could no more do anything to hurt Robin than he could Lisa. And it was tearing him apart.

"Michael?"

He tightened his arm around her, drawing her closer. "I know that too," he said finally, calmly.

•   •   •

"You didn't report in again last night," Daniel Stuart told his agent. "For God's sake, Skye, what's wrong with you?"

The man at the other end of the line cleared his throat. "Sorry, but there were a few—er, complications, and I had to move pretty fast."

"What kind of *complications*?" Daniel asked with deceptive mildness to his tone.

Remembering his mental rehearsals of this information, Skye realized that the practice had done no good at all; he still didn't know how to tell Daniel the whole story.

"Skye?"

"Yes, I'm still here."

"Then talk to me, dammit. What's going on?"

Skye drew an audible breath. "First, Michael has backup on this personal mission of his. The ladies I've been watching are now firmly in his corner, and they're pulling strings right and left. Things are happening even as we speak."

"What? Why would they—"

"Wait. I'll get to that later. They've set up a dandy diversion to draw Edward Sutton away from the yacht where he's holding Lisa along with several other girls."

There was a long silence, and then Daniel asked, "Is Sutton a slaver?"

"You caught that quicker than I did. Apparently he is. Seems he had several girls taken from a number of clubs a few days ago. He probably meant to ship them south before Michael came after Lisa, but there's a hell of a flap going on down here because of an alert for a drug shipment. The waters as well as the airways are hot. Sutton had to hole up and wait it out. Then one of the girls took her fate in her own hands and jumped ship. Michael fished her out of the water. She was able to tie Sutton to the club where she was snatched. And Michael, given the knowledge that Sutton could be on a yacht, lost no time in finding out—via Dane—the name and location of the yacht."

"My God," Daniel muttered.

"Yeah. My thoughts exactly. At any rate, the ladies I've been watching teamed up with Dane and headed for the Ten Thousand Islands very late last night."

"With Dane? What've you been doing?"

"Setting up the diversion at this end."

"You—"

"What else could I do, Daniel? I'm a trusted friend of Dane's, and somebody had to do the legwork."

Finally Daniel asked, "Do they know who you are?"

"Of course not."

There was another long silence, and then Daniel said, "I don't understand how your ladies got into this. The only one of the three who's even met Michael is Raven Long. What brought them tearing down there?"

"The connection wasn't with Michael, Daniel. They just went looking for him—and for Dane—because they needed information. A friend of one of them had turned up missing, and they were trying to find her."

Daniel Stuart stared blindly across his office, the instincts and intuition of a lifetime going off like a bell. "Skye, a friend of which one?"

"Teddy Steele."

"Not Robin," Daniel said hollowly.

"She's all right," Skye said. "At least . . . Oh, hell,

Daniel, she's with Michael. She was the one he pulled out of the water. And, apparently, she's determined to help him get his sister and the other girls off that yacht."

"Why didn't you contact me? I could have—"

"What? Flown down here? Things were moving so fast then, you wouldn't have had a hope in hell of stopping them. Between them, Raven and Dane had come up with a plan to cut the odds, and they put that plan into motion. I helped, because it seemed the best thing to do. Now Sutton's on his way to Miami, and Michael and Robin have a very talented group as backup."

"I'm coming down there," Daniel said.

"Yeah," Skye said. "I thought you would."

Six

Kneeling between Michael and Dane in the tangled undergrowth of the Maze, Robin stared across more than twenty feet of placid water at the *Dragon Lady*. The yacht was a peaceful sight, a couple of lights glowing dimly in starboard portholes, and a radio played quietly. Though it was only half past four, the cove was heavily shaded, and the yacht drifted in the shadows of twilight.

"How long?" Michael asked softly, tension evident in his voice.

Dane looked at his watch; in his free hand he held a small radio transmitter much more compact than a conventional walkie-talkie, and set to a frequency that would not interfere with normal radio transmissions. "Fifteen minutes," he answered, his voice equally low.

Robin, most of her mental energy involved in a determined battle against the cold fear crawling inside her, tried to keep her thoughts clear. The big cruiser, with Raven, Teddy, Kyle—and three of Sutton's guards—aboard was anchored just outside the cove, and all around the islands small and large fishing boats had swarmed in to try to win the unexpected prize money.

More than twenty minutes before, Raven and Teddy had hung over the side of the cruiser, dressed in scandalously brief swimsuits, and called out a laughing, pseudo-drunken invitation to the men on the yacht to join them for a party. After a brief, heated argument among Sutton's guards, three of them had launched an inflatable rubber dinghy and rowed over to the cruiser to accept the invitation. Robin, Michael, and Dane were waiting tensely for Raven to notify them that those party-inclined guards had been put out of commission.

Their best estimate was that there were four guards left on the yacht, at least two of whom, Raven had radioed, had dropped lines off the port side in a clear attempt to resemble fishermen.

"She should have radioed by now," Michael said.

"She will." Dane appeared unperturbed but kept one eye on his watch.

They could have moved against the yacht then, but neither Michael nor Dane had even considered doing so. They needed to know those guards would not be returning to the yacht, and they wanted to make certain Raven and her friends had no problems in subduing the men who had taken their bait.

Quietly, and still dividing his attention between his watch and the yacht, Dane said, "We should touch as little as possible on the yacht. Experts should be able to get a few of Sutton's fingerprints."

Michael gave him a sharp look. "You think this case will ever make it to court?"

"I think so," Dane replied calmly. "One of those thugs will be more than willing to talk if it means saving his own skin. The other ladies and I can testify to the fact that Sutton's been aboard the yacht. My credibility may be a little shaky," he added in a wry tone, "but those ladies are above reproach. And to top it all, you feds have been trying to get your hands on Sutton for some time now. This ought to do it."

Robin looked up at Michael. "Will it be enough for you?" she asked. "If Sutton goes to prison?"

After a moment Michael replied, "We'll see."

She knew what that meant. Once they found out how Lisa and the others had fared, Michael would decide whether to leave justice to the courts.

Dane's radio transmitter whispered softly, and they all heard Raven's muted but cheerful voice.

"Our guests are trussed up nicely. In five minutes all the guards left on the yacht should be on the port side, with their attention focused on us. Good luck, guys."

Some of the tension eased from Michael's face. Almost to himself, he murmured admiringly, "No wonder Hagen kept drafting those people."

"Hagen?" Robin asked, and it was Dane who replied.

"A federal honcho."

Michael gave him a look. "How do you know about him?"

Dane grinned. "I know a lot of things—and people —I'm not supposed to know."

"I'll bet," Michael remarked.

During the brief conversation they had been getting ready for the short, cautious swim to the yacht. The men were in swim trunks, with a number of waterproof equipment pouches belted around their waists; several items had come from Michael's boat, the remainder Dane and Raven had anticipated and brought along from Miami. They each carried an automatic pistol equipped with silencer, a long hunting knife, several short lengths of nylon rope, several pairs of the plastic handcuffs some federal authorities had begun using instead of metal ones, and compact tool kits—all just in case. In addition, Michael carried a coil of rope, knotted at intervals, with a rubber-tipped grappling hook on one end.

Robin wore a swimsuit borrowed from Teddy, with a similar belt containing a silenced automatic, several pairs of the handcuffs, and a Swiss Army knife. All of them carried an extra clip of bullets as a precaution, and each hoped not a single shot would be fired.

They were ready to execute their plan.

For Robin this situation was out of her worst nightmares. For almost half her life she had dreaded being put to this sort of test. She was an equal partner here, with her own role to play, her own set duties to perform, and if she failed in those duties, people could die.

She was a part of this by her own choice, but it was only Michael's matter-of-fact confidence in her that had allowed her to come this far. Dane's easy acceptance had helped, but it was Michael who knew only too well just how afraid she was. And with his own sister's life at stake . . .

Robin had never been so afraid, and she had never

been more determined to control her fear. The single most important realization Michael had forced her to face was that she *had* hedged the biggest bet of her life. She had failed an exam she should have passed easily, and that failure had marked her.

This was a test she had no intention of failing.

The side of the yacht nearest them, the starboard side, had been empty of activity as long as they had watched, but they waited until they heard Raven's clear, merry voice hailing the boat before they slipped into the water. Occupied with swimming as quietly as possible, they didn't catch much of the shouted conversation, but it appeared Raven was castigating them for having redneck friends who were making a shambles of her cruiser's cabin.

Her language was decidedly colorful, and seemed to amuse the men remaining on the yacht.

Reaching the yacht and moving carefully to a point where they could climb aboard unobserved by the guards, they trod water for a few moments, and then Michael very cautiously tossed the grappling hook up to the brass railing. It caught with a barely audible thud. Within seconds he was climbing the knotted rope quickly and easily.

Robin followed a moment later, not quite as quickly but with no wasted time or motion, and Dane came up after her.

They were passed against the wheelhouse, and the sounds of Raven's conversation with Sutton's men were clearer now; she was still giving them hell, and they were still laughing and encouraging her.

Robin found herself automatically reaching for her

gun and thumbing off the safety, holding it in a two-handed police grip at her right shoulder, pointed upward. She remained beside Michael as Dane eased toward the bow; until she got safely below, his job was to keep watch and make certain they weren't surprised by an approach from the front of the yacht. Then, when Robin was below, Dane would ease around to the port side and come at Sutton's men from the bow while Michael advanced on them from the stern.

Michael slipped along the wall of the wheelhouse, edging toward the stern until he could peer around and locate the entrance to the cabins below. Dane had provided a sketch of the complete layout of the yacht, and their movements once they got on board had been planned carefully.

Michael whispered, "The guards must be on the other side of the wheelhouse; I can't see them."

"I'm ready," Robin murmured.

Michael nodded once and exchanged places with her, holding his gun ready. "Three minutes, then Dane and I make our move. We'll be as quiet as possible. As soon as the guards topside are disarmed, I'll be heading below."

"Right."

"I'll cover you." He looked at her, his hard gray eyes lightening briefly in what was almost a smile. "Watch yourself, honey."

"You too." Robin managed a smile, drew a deep breath, then slipped around the side of the wheelhouse. Her bare feet made no sound on the deck, and it took only the space of heartbeats for her to cross the required space to the stairs leading below.

And this was the part of the plan that, by neces-

sity, had been loosely constructed. The best efforts
of Dane and the ladies had not told them how many
men, if any, might be below deck. They had theo-
rized that a ship of this size, with at least ten men
usually aboard, could have a cook, even a steward;
they had no way of knowing if one of the "guards"
was also the pilot, if one or more men had remained
below since the yacht had been under observation,
or if there was a crew in addition to Sutton's thugs.

Robin's job was to quickly and quietly secure the
area below deck and avoid a hostage situation; if
she missed even one man, that man could conceiva-
bly reach the kidnapped girls before Robin found
them. Since the men topside were heavily armed,
they posed the immediate danger. But if Michael
and Dane were unable to *quietly* disarm those men,
it would sound a warning to anyone below—which
was the sole reason she had a three-minute margin
in which to work.

Though her memories of her own time aboard the
yacht were clouded, Robin was reasonably sure there
had been no guard posted outside the cabin door
where she and the other girls had been held; the
drugs had apparently made that unnecessary. However, the night she had jumped ship, the storm had
required that all hands be topside and busy, which
had left her escape route clear.

But she couldn't be sure the situation was the
same now. She couldn't be sure about anything at
all.

She went down the stairs in a low crouch, gun
ready, tensely hesitating two steps from the bottom
to search the area visible from her position and
trusting Michael to watch the top of the stairs to

prevent her from being surprised from behind. At the bottom of the stairs began a long, narrow L-shaped hallway with several doors opening onto this first arm. The hallway was clear and well lighted. The gallery was just to the left of the stairway, the main cabin, a lounge, to the right, and then, according to Dane, a number of smaller cabins.

Robin had escaped the cabin located at the very end of the hallway, and Lisa had been somewhere close by. But the cabins in between had to be checked, one by one.

With the clock in her head ticking away the seconds, Robin came down the remaining two steps, and then pivoted, gun leveled, when she caught a glimpse of movement to her left.

"Don't move," she ordered very softly.

The man staring in horror at her gun didn't seem disposed to disobey the order. He was standing in the galley, preparations for a meal all around him, and he was old enough to have few illusions left to him.

"I'm not with them," he managed thickly. "I'm just the cook."

Robin didn't have time to reply to that, but she knew very well he had to be aware of the kidnapped girls and she wasn't feeling very charitable. "Turn around. Hands behind your back, feet apart. Wider!" She hadn't raised her voice, but the bite in it must have convinced the man she meant business; he followed the orders instantly.

Standing well back and making certain he remained off balance, Robin found the pair of handcuffs in her belt by touch and with one hand slipped them quickly over his wrists and tightened them.

Briefly she nudged him with the gun barrel. "On your knees." And when he had obeyed, she added, "I'm not alone here. If you make a sound, or try to move, you'll die. Understand?"

"Yes."

Her instinct told her he wouldn't make trouble; she had no time to gag him or take any other precautions. Easing cautiously back out into the hallway, she began to move away from the stairs, hardly aware that her police training was guiding her stance, every movement, barely conscious that her fear, for the first time, was a buried thing. All her senses were probing, listening, all her attention focused on what had to be done.

She listened briefly at each door, then opened one after another cautiously and scanned the interiors of the rooms. They proved to be empty; she left the doors open as she moved on to the next, and the next.

The clock in her head told her she had less than a minute left before Michael and Dane would make their move, and there were still doors to open, cabins to search.

Reaching the bend in the L-shaped hallway, she pressed flat against the wall and peered cautiously around. The hallway was empty. Five doors, the two of them nearest her, thank God, standing open. That left one door on each side of the hallway, and one at the end.

Robin opened the door on the left of the hallway first, and almost laughed aloud in relief. The tiny cabin was empty except for a girl in the single bunk. Obviously unconscious, she had dark blond hair and looked pale, but her breathing was audible.

Lisa.

Robin eased the door shut again and moved silently to the door at the end of the hall. There was no sound from within, and she opened the door slowly. The cabin was almost pitch dark; Robin remembered then that the portholes had been covered over by tightly closed lids from the outside, preventing any light from entering the cabin.

Senses flaring, probing the darkness, Robin stepped into the cabin and listened. Breathing. But, of how many people? There was a light switch; she reached for it cautiously.

And the silence was shattered, in a nerve-jarring instant, by the vicious chattering of an automatic weapon on the deck above.

Robin whirled, her heart in her throat, fear for Michael running through her body like ice. Before she could take more than a single step, the last unopened cabin door was yanked open, and a big, muscled man wearing only baggy trousers burst out into the hallway.

He wasn't heading for the stairs; he was going for Lisa's cabin. And he had a gun.

Robin didn't hesitate. In the instant granted to her she aimed by instinct and training and squeezed off a single shot. The silencer on her gun muted the usual violent sound so that all that emerged was a whistling pop, and the man's gun clattered to the floor as he fell back against the wall with a grunt of pain, holding a bleeding hand to his chest.

"You!" Malignant eyes fixed on her as Robin stepped carefully from the dark cabin, and he started to push himself away from the wall.

Robin remembered him; she owed most of her

bruises to him. She held the gun steady, aimed at the center of his chest, and met his gaze squarely as she spoke very quietly. "Don't."

Whether he would have given in to unreasoning rage became a moot point just then. Thudding footsteps rapidly approached them, and Michael came around the corner with his gun ready. His taut features eased instantly as he saw she was safe, and Robin felt a relief stronger than any she'd ever known make her knees go weak. He was unhurt.

With the increased odds against him, Robin's prisoner began muttering curses but made no further attempt to try brute strength against bullets.

Michael kept the man covered but addressed Robin quickly. "Lisa?"

She jerked her head toward the door without taking her eyes from the wounded man. "In there."

He kept his eyes and gun on the man until he could slip past him in the narrow hallway, then disappeared into Lisa's cabin.

Not three minutes later Dane came around the corner. Like Michael, he was whole and unhurt, gun ready. "We're batting a thousand topside," he said cheerfully but with a wary eye on the wounded man. "How about here?"

Robin managed a smile. "Here too. Could you take care of this one while I check on the other girls?"

"My pleasure." Dane smiled gently at the man. "Come on, sport, you can put a Band-Aid on that wound before you join your friends on deck."

Robin waited until they vanished around the corner, then turned quickly and went back into the darkened cabin. She flipped the light switch on, then sagged in relief when she saw two bunks and two cots occupied by four young women. All of them appeared to be unconscious, but otherwise seemed unharmed.

Taking up what little remained of the floor space in the cabin was a third cot, empty.

It was where Robin had experienced her nightmare.

An hour later all of Sutton's men, either tied up, unconscious, or both, had been transferred to the deck of the yacht, where those able to muttered curses and dire threats.

Both were ignored.

Michael, once satisfied that Lisa was unharmed barring her drugged state, helped Dane in the transfer of the men from the big cruiser. Kyle had brought the cruiser neatly into the cove and alongside the yacht, and the two vessels had been tied together for the duration.

Outside the cove the fishing tournament went on, the intent fishermen glad the commotion was over and not very concerned about what had happened in the cove. A single small boat had wandered into the cove, and the fisherman at the tiller, ignoring the spectacle of unconscious men being carried onto the yacht, asked Kyle, who was nearest to him, how the fishing was there. Kyle, never at a loss, told him politely that it was lousy and not likely to improve. He accepted her word, and putt-putted back out of the cove with an intense look on his face.

"Talk about being addicted to a sport," Dane muttered with a shake of his head, then went to stand guard over their prisoners while the others met in the hallway outside the two cabins still containing five unconscious, unaware young women.

"Michael, you're the only one of us with any kind of official status," Raven said. "It's your call. Do we radio the Coast Guard, or not?"

Michael was leaning against the doorjamb of Lisa's cabin, holding Robin's hand in his and glancing into the cabin from time to time to keep an eye on his sister. He was frowning a little, but despite that his face looked more at peace than Robin had ever seen it.

"How long is Sutton likely to be tied up in Miami?" he asked Raven slowly.

She smiled a little. "Days if we're lucky. Hours if we're not. If we call the Coast Guard in, they'll immediately contact the FBI, and *they* can contact the police in Miami once we make our statements implicating him in white slavery and kidnapping."

"That's no guarantee the police will be able to find him," Michael noted.

"No," she agreed. "And we don't know he has a contact schedule for his men on this boat. If so, and they miss the contact, he'll be alerted that something is wrong—and he could head for parts unknown before anybody gets near him. We could also have at least one of his men waiting on the coast with his launch who could alert him to any Coast Guard activity in the area." After a moment she added quietly, "Chances are fifty-fifty the police won't catch up to him for this before he's somehow alerted. On the other hand, I don't see that *your* chances of catching up to him right away are any better."

Michael glanced at Robin, smiled slightly, and nodded as he looked back at the former agent. "That was my reading. We do things legal from this point."

Robin felt relief sweep over her. She had been afraid Michael would be bent on getting his own justice, and he wasn't a man who would be easily stopped. At least he was willing to try the formal route first.

Raven was nodding. "Right. We have a doctor standing by at a private hospital in Fort Myers. These girls seem all right, but they've been heavily drugged for days and it's a good bet they're also dehydrated. They need to be under a doctor's care. We can transfer them to the cruiser, and Kyle and Teddy can have them in Fort Myers within hours. A small security team is also standing by to protect them— particularly Lisa—around the clock."

Michael's smile widened a bit. "I think I've asked this before, but is there anything you haven't thought of?"

She grimaced slightly. "I couldn't think of a way to catch Sutton red-handed without endangering the girls. Or a way to cut through the formalities. That means that you, Robin, Dane, and I have to remain here to do all the explaining. Dane and I because we can place Sutton on this yacht; you and Robin because of every other reason, including background information and the fact that Robin was kidnapped herself. We'll get enough flak as it is for having spirited the girls out of here, but we should get by on the grounds of needed medical attention."

"Lisa will be fine," Teddy assured him. "Someone will be with her all the time, and the moment she wakes up we'll tell her you're safe."

Michael glanced back into Lisa's cabin, and nodded. "Then let's do it."

It took almost another hour to move the unconscious girls onto the cruiser and make them comfortable, and then Kyle, with Teddy aboard, headed north toward Fort Myers.

The sun was beginning to set by then, and Michael went back across the Maze to bring his boat around to the cove after radioing the Coast Guard and explaining the situation. He had only just returned and tied up alongside the yacht when a Coast Guard cutter and a number of suspicious officials arrived.

Raven and Robin had managed to change into jeans and blouses before the cruiser had gone, and both Michael and Dane had found a moment to change as well, but none of them had eaten since lunch and they all found the questioning process extremely wearing. Darkness fell, and still the officials were trying to get every last detail, and questioning again all those they had.

They strongly disapproved of the fact that Robin had carried and used a gun she had no license for; they were bewildered by Raven's involvement; they spoke sternly about the kidnapped girls having been removed from the scene of their incarceration; they showed a marked, though veiled, hostility toward Dane; and Michael's credentials were viewed with open suspicion.

Yet none of them was allowed to leave the yacht or to contact anyone.

By the third hour, though all four were accustomed to dealing with police and officials in one way or another, Michael, Robin, Raven, and Dane were all conscious of threadbare patience.

The situation might have continued until long into the night, but there was the sound of an approaching engine, an abrupt flurry of footsteps on the deck above—and a deep, commanding voice began to take charge with a vengeance.

Robin, sitting with the others in the lounge as they were being questioned—again—by two FBI men, sat up suddenly with a jerk, her eyes widening.

"Good Lord," she exclaimed.

Michael, who had also recognized the voice, kept his arm around her and met her startled gaze with a smile. "I figured he'd be showing up sooner or later."

"You know?" She blinked, then began to smile. "He's your boss, isn't he?"

" 'Fraid so," Michael confessed. "I made the connection with the names a while back, but because I hadn't been in touch with him since before you and I met—"

"You didn't feel the need to tell me?"

"Something like that."

"What are we talking about?" Raven asked with interest, ignoring the suspicious stares of the FBI men.

Before Robin could reply, a tall, powerful-looking, silver-haired man in his late fifties strode into the room and sent a single sweeping glance around the room out of vivid green eyes. If the eagle's glare paused on Robin for an instant, it wasn't obvious, and passed on immediately to the two FBI agents. So rapier-sharp was the glare that no one in the room would have been surprised if those special agents had begun looking for wounds on their bodies.

"What the hell," he asked politely, "is going on here?"

"This is a federal investigation," the younger of the two agents began importantly, and was cut off.

"It looks to me like a bumbling investigation," Daniel Stuart said, still very politely. "I was notified hours ago, yet I find when I arrive that no word has been sent to the Miami police, no effort made to locate and arrest Edward Sutton, and if this is your idea of how to handle a crime scene, all I can add is you boys are going back in training."

"Look, I don't know who you are—" The younger one again began to bluster, but the older of the two began to look queasy.

Daniel reached into an inner pocket and produced a small folded case, which he opened and held out before the two men at eye level. Very softly he asked, "Any questions?"

Both agents had stiffened. "No, sir," the older one said while the other just looked miserable.

Snapping the case shut and returning it to his pocket, Daniel said, "Fine. You men are relieved. Leave your notes—I assume you took some?—and any relevant information with my men up on deck. Then get your butts back to your office and wait."

A moment later Robin said, "I've never seen grown men *scurry* before." She barely made it to her feet before being engulfed in a bear hug, and added breathlessly, "Hi, Dad."

"Hi, yourself," he returned, his voice a bit thickened now with a different emotion. "Next time you plan to steal ten years off my life, would you at least *tell* me first?"

Robin hugged him back, then smiled as he held her at arm's length and looked her up and down. "I had to prove a few things to myself first," she confessed. "I'm sorry, Dad."

It was difficult for her to keep her voice steady. Seeing her father for the first time in years, it had hit her with a shock just how thoroughly her past failures had disrupted—and nearly destroyed—her life. She had cut herself off from the father she adored because, as Michael had said, she had hedged a vital bet and had subsequently labeled herself a failure.

She would never do so again.

"As long as you're all right." He hugged her once more, then released her and shook hands with Michael. "And the next time *you* go tearing off alone, I'll dock your pay," he told the younger man with mock severity.

"I'll remember that," Michael said.

"Glad to hear Lisa's safe," Daniel added more seriously.

"I can't take the credit."

Before the others could react, Daniel turned to them and said, "Hello, Dane," and then smiled at Raven. "I've been looking forward to meeting you, Mrs. Long. I've heard a great deal about you."

"From whom?" she asked curiously, offering her hand.

Daniel accepted it with more of a bow then a handshake, a gesture he carried off well. "From Hagen among others."

She shook her head with a smile. "I guess the

intelligence community is even smaller than I thought. Please, make it Raven."

Michael was looking from Daniel to Dane, a speculative gleam in his eye. "I wasn't aware you two knew each other," he offered.

It was Dane who responded, in a vague tone, while avoiding Michael's gaze. "Federal honchos need information too."

"Uh-huh," Michael said.

Before that could go any further, Daniel said, "You all must be exhausted. Raven, you rented a house on the coast, right?"

"Right," she answered, not surprised by his knowledge.

"Why don't all of you go back there and get some rest. We'll finish up here, and I'll come to the house in the morning with your statements ready to sign."

No one bothered to ask if he knew where the house was.

"Wait a minute," Robin said, gazing at her father. "I have to know something. That ID you showed those guys—what was it?"

Daniel pulled the small case out of his pocket and handed it to her, smiling faintly.

All four of them looked at the case, and it was Robin who said in astonishment, "*Director* of the FBI? Since when?"

"Since a couple of days ago. It hasn't been announced yet."

"Congratulations, Daniel," Michael offered.

"Thanks."

Raven looked patently relieved, a reaction that was explained by her rueful words. "I was always afraid

Hagen would get that job, and God help America if he did."

Daniel cleared his throat. "He was being considered. And he doesn't know I've been appointed yet."

Raven's relieved expression became blissful. "How nice. May I give him the news? Face-to-face, so I can see his reaction?"

Chuckling, Daniel said, "You may tell him Wednesday morning; it's being announced that afternoon."

"I'm looking forward to it," Raven said with a grin.

When the *Black Angel* slipped out of the cove a few minutes later, she left behind her a yacht lighted from bow to stern and crawling with federal agents, the Coast Guard cutter that Daniel and his men had arrived on—the first one had left—and a number of mildly puzzled fishermen still hoping to land a prize-winning catch by midnight.

Aboard the *Angel* were four very tired but still keyed-up people, all feeling the physical letdown of diminishing adrenaline and the emotional high of having successfully beaten the odds.

Michael was at the wheel, with Dane keeping him company, and Robin and Raven were on deck enjoying the cool night air.

"I like your father," Raven told Robin decisively. "And he's a pleasure to deal with. Especially after Hagen."

"Can you tell me about Hagen?" Robin asked curiously. "Dane said he was a federal honcho, but—"

"Dane said that?" Raven laughed softly. "It shouldn't surprise me, I suppose. He seems to have an ear to the ground when it comes to intelligence operations.

Sure, I'll tell you about Hagen; I stopped keeping that man's secrets when he nearly got me killed."

So she told Robin the story, beginning with her own involvement with Hagen and touching rapidly on the various events she, her husband, and their friends had become entangled in due to Hagen's deft manipulation.

By the time the *Angel* bumped gently against the long pier jutting out from Raven's rented house, Robin was torn between horrified fascination and the intense desire to meet this Hagen before somebody strangled him.

That, Raven told her, was a common reaction.

Seven

The house Raven and her friends had rented was a big, sprawling place, fifty yards from the sandy beach and set high on massive pilings. It was isolated, but the lights they had left burning early that morning gave it a welcoming air.

Michael drew his *Black Angel* up to the long pier, and they all helped in tying her up before heading toward the house. Steps led up to a big wooden deck, where French doors and floor-to-ceiling glass provided the central den with a clear view of the ocean. The place was comfortably furnished and equipped, Raven told them, with every necessity except food; she and her friends had brought that along with them.

All four worked together in preparing a casual meal in the kitchen, talking idly, still winding down from the tensions and activity of the day. They had barely finished cleaning up afterward when the phone rang.

Raven answered, and after a short conversation hung up and turned to the others with a smile. "Kyle says the girls are fine; they reached the hospital without a problem, and the security team is in place. The doctor told her it'll be days before all the drugs are out of their systems, and he wants to keep them under observation. Michael, he said to tell you that Lisa wasn't hurt at all—not even a bruise. It'll be at least a couple of days before she knows what's going on around her. Also, they have a very good trauma specialist to help all the girls deal with what happened to them."

"Thank you, Raven," Michael said quietly. He was sitting beside Robin one of the two couches. Glancing from Raven to Dane, he added, "Both of you. And, Raven, if I don't see Teddy and Kyle before you head back to New York—"

She waved that away. "Don't mention it. Now, there are four bedrooms and four baths in this place. Everybody take your pick. I'm beat, and I'm turning in."

Dane, lounging in a chair, said, "Me too. I've used muscles today I didn't know I had."

Robin, who had noticed a number of well-defined muscles when they'd all been running around in bathing suits earlier, eyed him in amusement. But she said nothing; if she had learned anything about Michael's world, she had learned that things were rarely as they appeared on the surface.

When they were alone, she looked at Michael, conscious of the tension still remaining in his lean body. She knew intuitively that he found it difficult to relax after today and all the days since Lisa had been kidnapped. It was hardly surprising, she thought, considering what kind of strain he'd been under through all this.

"Why don't we take a walk on the beach?" she suggested lightly. "I don't think either one of us is ready to sleep yet."

"Good idea."

He took his gun with him, worn this time in a shoulder holster; it didn't surprise Robin, nor did she feel a need to comment on his caution.

The tide was going out, and they walked over the wet, firmly packed sand just below the high-water mark. There was a full moon reflecting off the water, and a soft breeze blowing.

"I haven't thanked you yet," he said suddenly after they'd walked for a time in silence.

"There's no need to."

"Yes, there is." He reached for her hand and held it tightly. "I know what it cost you, going down that hall on the yacht alone. I know it was—something out of your nightmares."

"It's funny," she mused, "but it wasn't like that. I thought it would be. And I was afraid. But once we were on the boat, there just . . . didn't seem to be time enough to be afraid. Except when I heard someone on deck start shooting. What happened?"

"One of the guards took a few shots at Dane. But when he saw I had him covered, he dropped the gun fast."

"That gave me a bad moment," she confessed. "Then that man tore out of the cabin, and there wasn't time to think. He was making for Lisa, and I had to stop him."

After a moment Michael said, "I think those demons have finally stopped chasing you."

Robin knew there was one last demon at her heels, one final test she had to pass, but she wasn't ready for it just yet. And she wasn't ready to talk about it to Michael. "I owe you a lot," she said instead.

"You owe me nothing." His voice was steady. "If there was ever a debt, it was more than paid today."

They walked in silence for several minutes, and then Robin asked the question that had been haunting her. "What about us, Michael? Where do we go from here?"

He stopped, faced her. The moonlight painted half his face in stark relief, left the rest in shadow. He was half there, curiously incomplete. The highlights and shadows stole all expression, leaving his face a mask. She didn't—couldn't—know what he was thinking.

"It's tomorrow," she said. "And I still love you."

His hands found her shoulders, fingers moving gently in an absent, probing touch. "What about that story you were going to write?"

Robin drew a deep breath. "I got too involved. I lived that story; I can't write about it. Not yet."

He was silent for a moment, then spoke almost tentatively. "I'll probably be at loose ends for a while. With Daniel leaving to assume the FBI directorship, there's bound to be a restructuring of our agency. Until the dust settles, I won't be given a new assignment. Even then I have time coming to me; I want to spend some of that with Lisa, make sure she's all right."

Robin waited, wondering if he could feel or sense her growing tension. The hands on her shoulders tightened.

"Stay with me," he said huskily. "For a while, at least."

She went into his arms silently, conscious of relief mixed with pain. He was still holding a part of himself back, she knew, still guarding the vulnerable place in his heart where wounds never healed and the ache lasted forever. Even knowing no more than bits and pieces of his past, Robin couldn't blame him for that.

She couldn't blame him, but it hurt. He trusted her, but he didn't trust her love for him. And Robin didn't know how much time she would have to convince him.

But, for now it was enough. She had been afraid that Michael would try to send her away, and anything else was preferable to that. Anything.

With one mind they started back toward the house, Michael's arm around her shoulders and hers around his waist. Neither said anything more about the future because there was nothing more to be said.

When they were inside again, Michael said, "I'll lock up down here."

Robin nodded, heading for the open stairs to the right of the den. There were two sets of stairs because the upper floor was divided in half with two bedrooms and a bath looking down on each side of the den/kitchen combination below. Raven and Dane had taken the two bedrooms to the left, leaving the other side for Robin and Michael.

Robin had been reunited with her luggage, thanks to Teddy and her friends' thoughtfulness in bringing it with them from Miami, and she'd brought an overnight bag with her while leaving the rest on

Michael's boat. The others had also brought with them some kind of overnight bag.

She went upstairs while Michael checked the doors and windows downstairs, and arbitrarily chose the oceanside bedroom. Like the other rooms, it was spacious and airy, with a wide, comfortable bed already made up. Robin decided on a shower, conscious of the residue of salt from her earlier swim, and unpacked only her toiletries bag to take into the bathroom.

She stepped under the warm spray with relief, remembering with some amusement the tiny bathroom on Michael's boat where she had burned her bridges. This shower stall was considerably larger, the entire room was, in fact, and a far more ideal place for an attempted seduction.

Robin was washing her hair when she saw, through the steam-fogged glass door, Michael come in and begin shaving at the vanity. It felt right, neither of them self-conscious, casual together even in intimacy. She thought about that, happy with the idea, but realizing a few minutes later that where there was intimacy and desire, "casual" was a fleeting thing.

She was even happier about that.

Michael slipped into the stall with her, eyes darkened and intent, and took the bar of soap from her. "Let me," he stated a bit roughly.

Robin couldn't take her eyes off him even as her body responded instantly and wildly to his touch, and she reached for him. He seemed to be memorizing her, tracing every curve and hollow with his strong hands, and she found a new delight in the sensation of slick muscles under her fingers. The normally unthinking, automatic actions of soaping and rinsing became a series of caresses, hers and his, seeking, slippery touches while the water beat down on them.

Michael tossed the bar of soap out of the shower and pulled her into his arms suddenly, their bodies sliding together in a sensuous friction as he covered her mouth with his in a deep, almost violent kiss.

Robin felt his hand tangle in her hair, holding her head firmly while his mouth took hers and his tongue probed and possessed, the building heat in her writhing like something alive. It was different from their previous lovemaking, this driving hunger of his, and she realized dimly that a part of his earlier guardedness had stemmed from what had then lain ahead of them. He had shut a large part of himself off from her because that trained, dangerous part of him, by necessity, had concentrated on rescuing his sister and the other girls.

But not now. Danger past, his mind was fully on her, and if he was still guarded, it was a final wall, the deepest possible shield protecting his heart. Desire was uppermost, almost uncontrolled, hunger fierce and total.

And Robin responded to his need with a burning craving of her own. She could hardly breathe, and her legs were weak, shaking, her hands trembling as she helplessly stroked his shoulders, his back. Then his hands slid down to her buttocks, lifting her against him, off her feet, and a moan caught in her throat.

Michael was scarcely aware of the water beating

down on them. Her flesh tasted of soap and natural sweetness, and he couldn't get enough of her. The soft, unconscious sounds she made drove his desire higher and higher, fogging his mind with a heat that was burning him. He lifted her higher, his mouth seeking her throat and then her breasts, finding nipples that were wet and sweet, tight and hard with wanting him.

Robin held on to him fiercely, feeling the cool wall against her back, feeling his body and his mouth. She was aching all over, burning, and if they could have opened the shower stall and tumbled immediately into bed, it wouldn't have been fast enough for her. Her legs parted and lifted, wrapping around his waist.

"Now," she whispered hoarsely, the word echoing her desperate need. "Now, Michael, please . . ."

With a hoarse sound he buried himself in her, pinning her to the wall with the first deep thrust. For an instant, a heartbeat, he was still, his body rigid against her and inside her as he fought to control his wild need. But control was impossible, and his body recognized that long before his fogged mind could. His powerful thrusts were an erotic assault, and she whimpered with the incredible pleasure of it.

The soft, tight sheath of her body was a velvet clasp around him, driving Michael to the edge and over. He found her mouth, wild and rough, catching her faint cries so that they mingled with his own hoarse sounds. He wanted more of her, all of her, wanted to merge himself with her so completely that she would never be rid of him.

She stiffened against him and uttered a ragged moan, clinging tightly to his shoulders as waves of ecstasy jolted through her body. The inner ripples of her pleasure caught him in a tight, rhythmic caress, holding him deeply inside her, and he groaned wildly, dying a little, violently alive as his own release shattered the unbearable tension.

Robin came back to an awareness of her surroundings slowly, conscious again of the shower still beating down on them. She was shaking, as if aftershocks of that incredible passion still rippled through her, and he was as well. Her legs released him finally, sliding down over his hips and legs, and he let her down slowly until she was on her feet again. But he continued to hold her close, both of them leaning against the cool wall of the shower stall and each other.

"Lord, Robin," he said, turning her face up and kissing her gently, deeply.

She managed a shaky laugh. "We could have drowned," she told him. "Or fallen and broken our necks."

Michael smiled a little, his eyes still dark and intent. "But we didn't."

"No." Astonishingly Robin realized that neither her desire nor Michael's had been completely satisfied. Weary as both had undoubtedly been, their lovemaking had energized them. She cleared her throat, adding, "There's a bed in the next room, you know."

Michael reached to turn off the shower, still smiling. "Yes, I noticed that."

Conscious of her weak legs and trembling body,

but also aware of glowing embers inside her, Robin followed him from the shower stall, both reaching for towels.

Much later, lying close beside Michael in the comfortable bed, the sheet drawn over their cooling bodies, Robin thought, *It's the middle of the night.* But she was still wide awake, reluctant to sleep, afraid of losing . . . something.

And he was awake beside her, one arm around her, his fingers toying with her hair. She wondered if he was afraid of losing something too.

"Michael?"

"Hmmm?"

The room was lit only by moonlight streaming through the big windows, stark and sly. "You said—when we were talking about love that didn't last, you said it had happened to you."

He didn't tense or draw away, but she could feel as well as hear a rough sigh escape him. "Yes, I did."

"Can you . . . will you tell me about it?"

"There isn't much to tell."

Robin was silent.

He sighed again and drew her closer, almost as if in apology for his brusque tone. And his voice changed, becoming quiet and calm as he spoke again. "It was along time ago, Robin. Years ago. It doesn't matter now."

"Yes, it does," she whispered.

He was silent for a long moment, then told her the story without expression—and without apology.

"I was assigned to infiltrate a smuggling ring. It

was a tight, well-organized operation, and we didn't have a hope of getting in until the sister of one of the men involved tipped us; she had just found out what her brother was into and believed—rightly in their case—that he didn't know how serious the situation was. In fact, he was considered a weak link in the chain, and the other men were about to take steps to get rid of him.

"The sister insisted on getting involved in my operation, hoping to get her brother out of the mess alive. And she wouldn't take no for an answer. She had made her own involvement a condition in telling us what we had to know, and I had an inexperienced partner to cope with."

Robin listened silently, seeing the parallels and wondering if she really wanted to hear this.

"The men involved were tough and paranoid; we were in danger every second of our exposure, things were moving very fast, and there was no time to think. She and I had nothing in common except the situation, but that seemed to be everything. It was bigger than both of us, and it carried us along."

Robin knew, but asked anyway. "What happened?"

"The worst possible thing—and the most inevitable—we became lovers, Robin. And it was *real*. For a while. Until all the shouting was over and the dust settled. Her brother made it, and turned state's evidence against the others. The assignment was completed successfully, and we came out with our skins intact. It was over."

"You and she . . ."

Michael was silent for a moment, then answered with no change in his unemotional tone. "That was over too. She said it was still real for her, but it wasn't for me. I hurt her, Robin. I had believed I loved her, but the situation was responsible for those feelings. Once it was over, the feelings were gone. She wasn't in my head or my heart. I didn't even want her anymore. And I hurt her."

Robin felt her throat tighten, felt the stinging heat of tears behind her eyes. She wondered with a throb of pain if she was listening to the epitaph of her own love. And she realized now what Michael had tried to protect her from in the beginning. Not the fleeting reality of her feelings—but the fleeting reality of *his*.

She spoke steadily past the tightness of her throat. "What happened to her?"

"She left." He sounded restless now. "Went back home. Somewhere in the Midwest, I think."

Robin found it impossible to say anything else. *Did you tell her you loved her, Michael? You haven't told me. And I don't even know if that's good or bad.* He had offered her no false promises, had even warned her that she would be hurt. He had said she wouldn't love him "tomorrow" when what he had really meant was that he probably wouldn't feel anything for her, not even desire.

He moved suddenly, lifting himself on one elbow and gazing down at her with somber eyes, the moonlight painting his face starkly in a mask of control. "I want to tell you that this time it'll be different. I *want* to, Robin. But I can't. I don't know. I can't lie to you about it. I don't know what I'm feeling—except that I want you with me. *And* I don't want to hurt you."

Her hand lifted with a need beyond reason, touching his face, tracing the hard line of his jaw and feeling a muscle leap under her fingers. That guarded part of him, she thought, unwilling to define his own feelings, wary of having them disappear like smoke through his fingers.

It almost broke her heart.

"Don't," he whispered suddenly in an anguished sound, his head lowering until he could kiss her. His hands framed her face, thumbs gently brushing her tears away. "Don't let me hurt you, honey. I don't think I could stand it."

Robin was beginning to understand him now, even in her own pain. He wasn't a man who could wound another and walk away uncaring; Michael cared too much. He bore the scars of every hurt inflicted on him, by him. And that was why he was a loner, avoiding relationships, wary of friends. Because one of life's ironies was that this caring man lived in a world where people were often hurt, sometimes killed, and always capable of betrayal.

"Robin, don't," he whispered, tasting her pain as his tongue caught a silvery tear near her temple.

She couldn't stand it, couldn't bear thinking about it anymore; she wanted to block it all out until it didn't hurt, at least for now. Pushing suddenly against his shoulders, she rolled with him until he was on his back and she was above him. Feverishly her lips moved down his neck and over his chest, trying to fill her mind and senses with him, hoarding memories against a possible long, cold future without him.

Michael caught his breath and went still, his fingers tangling in her hair as his body began responding to the velvet touch of her lips, the hot darts of her tongue. His heart began thudding with greater force and speed in his chest, and sensual tension seeped into him as his belly knotted, his loins hardened.

He knew he had already hurt her, and this was a bittersweet pleasure at first, a pleasure that was almost pain. But passion knew only desires, not fears, and soon he was totally caught up in the building response of his body to her hunger.

Robin's tears dried, and the ache loosened around her heart, spreading outward in heating ripples as desire replaced pain. She became completely involved in what she was doing, fascinated and enthralled in this first opportunity to explore his body. They had been so intimate, yet she hadn't fully realized how her senses could expand so immeasurably in the driven desire to give pleasure.

She could feel her whole awareness open up, until she was conscious of every breath he drew, until the clean, faintly salty taste of his skin drew her compulsively. His body was hard and hot, muscles taut, his breathing ragged. Her mouth found a flat nipple in the nest of black hair and drew it inward, her tongue teasing until he groaned softly and shuddered.

And there was, faintly, a sense of astonished power at the realization of how she affected him. A stroke of her hand made him tense even more and shiver, and her mouth seemed to burn him wherever it touched. Robin was fascinated, and her own desire was spiraling in a wild ascent.

Her hands and lips trailed down his body, exploring avidly, learning him completely. She was barely aware of her own pounding heart and shallow breathing, too conscious of his response to her touch to be concerned with her own. She felt driven to please him, uninhibited and glorying in the freedom of it.

If Robin had been thinking at all, she would have understood another need driving her, but it would occur to her only later: It was his will standing between them, his forceful strength and sure self-knowledge—and she was trying to break down that wall.

With every caress, every touch of her lips, she was driving him relentlessly toward the brink, passionately stealing every last atom of his conscious will, taking his strength in the only way she knew, the only way it was possible to steal from a strong man and make him powerless to control the need she had ignited. She was almost sobbing as the wild, compulsive desire gripped her, mindless in her need to break down the barrier between them.

And something broke, whether it was that barrier or simply Michael's control. With a harsh, ragged groan, he pulled her up above him, guiding her with fierce insistence until she settled down slowly and they were fully joined. She looked down at him with clouded green eyes, her breath escaping quickly from between parted lips.

A siren, her witch's eyes sultry, her smile a Madonna's.

Michael let her set the tempo, gritting his teeth at the shattering pleasure as she moved slowly, her body sheathing his in tight heat, the friction almost unbearable. He could feel shivers of pleasure running up and down his spine, feel the taut ache of muscles held rigid in a kind of blissful paralysis. He could hardly breathe, his heart pounding out of control, his mind hazy, emotions tangled in wild confusion.

The pleasure built in waves of intensity, higher and higher, a slow, throbbing, aching violence, a storm trapped inside them and raging with the need to escape. Until Michael couldn't bear it any longer, her slow, lingering seduction stole more than his will. His hard hands guided her lips as he surged beneath her, taking over as they both plunged head-long toward release.

And when they found it at last, neither could make a sound. The eruption of that shattering storm held them in a stark, blinding silence that was eternal, that was a heartbeat, that was more than a tiny death.

Robin collapsed on his chest, dazed, limp. She couldn't have moved to save her life, and Michael's reaction was the same. His arms held her, but with no strength, his heart still thudding beneath her cheek as his chest rose and fell jerkily.

Robin felt peace envelop her finally, felt herself drifting toward sleep as her consciousness slipped away. But in her last moments of awareness, she realized at last why both she and Michael had been so energized, why they had made love so passionately and long past the point that sheer physical exhaustion should have claimed them both.

Both of them could have died. So easily. A foot put wrong, a minute slip, a tiny mistake. They could have died, and hadn't. They had survived against all odds. They had even triumphed. And though their lovemaking had been the result of simple desire and need, deeper, more primitive emotions had driven them far beyond that.

They were *alive*. A primal awareness of survival insisted on a celebration of that fact, and there was no more intimate, primitive testament to the living spirit than the act of two people joining their bodies, minds, and souls together.

It was an affirmation of life itself.

Sunlight woke Robin, and she lifted her head to blink toward the window in faint annoyance. Then a niggling uneasiness told her the sun shouldn't have been shining so brightly through the window, and she pondered that. West. That was it; the window faced the ocean, which was to the west.

It was afternoon. Late afternoon.

Satisfied with the conclusion, she lowered her head to rest once again on Michael's chest and closed her eyes. A moment later, however, her head lifted again, eyes wide in startled recollection. Late afternoon. And her father had said he'd be there in the morning! She looked back over her shoulder, relieved to see the door firmly closed.

Then, looking back at her pillow, she swallowed a giggle. *I hope nobody decided to find out if we were alive in here,* she thought giddily.

Obviously neither she nor Michael had moved an inch since sleep had claimed them sometime before dawn. She was lying comfortably next to him, and since the sheet had slipped to the floor during her explorations of his body, they were both gloriously uncovered.

Awake now, Robin looked down at Michael's sleeping face and felt her heart turn over. Completely relaxed and unguarded, he looked years younger and almost painfully vulnerable. If she ever saw his face like that when he was awake and aware, she knew suddenly it would be because he loved her.

Pushing the thought aside, Robin moved carefully to slip from his loose embrace. He made a soft sound in his throat but didn't move, and she was able to get off the bed without waking him. Standing beside the bed, she stretched, then winced as muscles twinged in protest. Her stiffness could have been due to the exertions of the day before—or those of the night. She smiled as she mentally decided on the blame.

She found a change of clothes in her overnight bag, then went softly into the bathroom to wash her face and brush her teeth, still trying not to wake him. When she emerged from the bathroom a few minutes later, she was dressed in shorts and a blouse, and Michael was still asleep.

She opened the bedroom door and eased from the room, closing it quietly behind her. The house was silent, and it wasn't until she was nearly at the bottom of the stairs that she saw her father. He was standing out on the deck gazing at the ocean, but turned as she saw him and came back into the house.

"Uh—hi, Dad," she managed.

"Hello," he returned politely. "There's coffee in the kitchen."

Robin headed in that direction, wondering if she looked as though she needed it. "Where is everyone?" she asked.

Her father sat down at the breakfast bar and lifted his own coffee cup. "Gone. Dane had to get back to Miami, and Raven headed toward Fort Myers to rejoin her friends."

"How did they—"

"I called a Coast Guard cutter to ferry Dane; Raven took the one I arrived in. It's back at the pier now; I'll have to be going in a couple of hours."

"Oh." Robin sipped her coffee and tried to get a grip on herself, a bit unsettled beneath her father's steady, amused gaze. "Sorry we—I—slept so late. Must have been more tired than I thought."

Daniel Stuart nodded gravely. "Must have been. Raven left the key to the house, by the way; she said to tell you it's rented through next weekend, and to make yourself at home."

Robin leaned back against the counter and avoided his eyes. "Oh. Well, I'm not sure . . . that is, it was very nice of her," she finished lamely.

"Yes, it was," he agreed, seemingly more amused with every passing second.

She fidgeted a moment, then asked, "Have they caught Sutton yet?"

"No, but it's just a matter of time."

"Do you know how Lisa and the other girls are doing?" she asked him.

"I talked to the hospital this morning. They're all doing fine, though still unconscious. How about you?" he asked quietly.

She was a little startled, until she remembered that he had to know she'd been kidnapped herself. "I'm fine. No nightmares. I guess helping the other girls exorcised my demons."

He nodded, looking at her steadily. "That was a tough thing you did, Robin. I hope you know I'm very proud of you."

She felt her throat close up, and heard the words

emerge without thought. "I'm sorry I failed at the academy, Dad."

Daniel was shaking his head. "You didn't fail me, if that's what you've been worried about."

Robin hesitated, then told him, finally, about her lifelong battle against fear. And about how Michael had forced her to understand that—and herself. The words emerged painfully but honestly, and when she finished, Daniel came around the bar and embraced her.

"You should have told me," he said gently.

"I couldn't. Not then. I didn't even understand it myself, until Michael made me."

Her father looked down at her for a moment, then said in a quiet voice, "You love him."

"Yes. Yes, I do."

Eight

Sitting on the couch, Robin was half turned to face her father as both sipped coffee. She had been honest with her father, as she had been with him for most of her life; only her tangled fears had ever been kept from him. "I don't know about the future," she was saying quietly. "Or even if there is one for Michael and me. He's been very honest about that."

Daniel was watching her steadily, reading the play of emotions across her expressive face. "Yes, Michael's an honest man. And a good man. But, Robin, he isn't a safe man. Not a safe man to love, I mean. His life will always be dangerous."

"I know that." She managed a smile, and her tone was filled with wry understanding. "Don't forget, my father's the same kind of cop."

That particular "cop" nodded slightly. "But is that the life you want for yourself? The kind of man you want? It's important for you to be sure, honey, before you commit yourself. The longer you stay with him, the harder it'll be on you both if it doesn't work out."

She sighed. "Everything's happened so fast. But I haven't had any doubts, Dad, not since I realized I loved him. And I can't put a time limit on this, tell myself I'll bail out if it starts to hurt too much. I don't have a choice; I never did. I'll stay with him as long as he wants me."

Daniel smiled faintly, the almost bittersweet look of a man who knows his daughter is a woman grown and beyond his control. "Yeah, I thought you'd say that. In fact, I was sure you would. I saw the way you looked at him. But I had to ask. Fatherly duty, you understand."

Robin smiled, loving him very much indeed. "You were always good at explaining whenever you said or did something for that reason. Fatherly duty. When you grounded me for a month, or took away my car keys because I'd done something wrong. Or told me I couldn't date Andrew McKay because he was a budding juvenile delinquent, and you'd be damned if you had to get your own daughter out of jail at one in the morning. It was your fatherly duty to avoid that, you said."

"You didn't believe me," he said, pained.

"Oh, I believed you. I just didn't like it. Even cops' daughters have to go through their rebellious teen-age years. Mine were no worse than anyone else's." She lifted an eyebrow at her father. "Besides, four sons had spoiled you. By the time I came along, you were due to be shaken up."

Daniel continued to look pained, but there was laughter in his green eyes. "Well, dammit, nobody warned me daughters were different. Your mother tried, but I have to admit I didn't know what she was talking about. It wasn't until you started wearing eye shadow that it really hit me. And by then it was too late to lock you in a tower; I'd already taught you how to handle guns. All I could do was bite my nails and keep the front porch light on."

Robin laughed, remembering dates bringing her home and walking her to the door under that bright yellow glare. Then, sobering, she said, "I've always heard that most fathers find it difficult to accept a man in their little girl's life. I guess I never really thought about it, though."

"It isn't easy," Daniel confessed wryly. "You think about fixing ponytails and tying shoelaces and putting Band-Aids on skinned knees . . ." His hand reached out for hers, holding it strongly. "And then you glance up one day, and see a beautiful young woman with hair spray and high heels and the odd run in her stocking. Looking at another man the way she used to look at you, trusting and adoring."

Robin blinked back sudden tears. "So how are you handling it?"

He smiled, his own eyes bright. "The best way I can. By reminding myself that I raised you to think for yourself, to make your own decisions. And by admitting to myself that a man in the life of a beautiful young woman is inevitable. Just like death and taxes." He laughed a little, shaking his head, then sobered abruptly. "In all honesty, honey, I couldn't have picked a better man for you."

She laughed shakily. "Then cross your fingers and hope I can pull it off."

"I have faith in you." He squeezed her hand and then released it. "You come from a long line of fighters, and not one of them ever gave up. You'll get what you want."

"I hope you're right." Her attention distracted by sounds from upstairs, she listened intently, then added, "I hear the shower; Michael's awake."

"Mmm." Daniel nodded toward the coffee table, where a sheaf of papers lay. "You'd better read and sign your statement. Your father or not, I have to do most things by the book. And then . . . I need to talk to Michael alone before I go."

"So I should take a walk on the beach?" she asked dryly, sorting her statement from the others and picking it up.

"If you wouldn't mind. Sorry, honey, but it's business."

Robin was reading her typed statement, and responded absently. "It's all right, Dad. I don't mind." But when she had signed the statement and moved toward the French doors leading to the deck, she hesitated and looked back at him.

He could read her expressive face easily. Quietly he said, "Your relationship with Michael is your business, honey, not mine. I won't interfere."

"Thanks, Dad," she said.

A few minutes later, when Michael came down the stairs wearing only a pair of jeans, Daniel met him with a calm look. "Michael, there's coffee in the kitchen."

"Thanks." He glanced around. "Robin?"

"Walking on the beach. I asked her to. I wanted to talk to you alone."

After a slight hesitation Michael nodded and went to fix himself a cup of coffee.

On the couch Daniel gazed out at the view and waited placidly.

Robin walked a good distance up the beach, uncertain of how much time her father needed. It was almost an hour later when she neared the house again, and saw her father and Michael come out onto the deck. By the time she reached the pier, her father was waiting for her there, while out in the water and tied up across from Michael's boat, the big Coast Guard cutter started its powerful engines.

"Come with me, Robin," Daniel urged, his eyes intent. "We have a lot of catching up to do, you and I."

She was a little surprised by his words, and felt vaguely uneasy. "I'll come see you once you've settled into your new office, Dad."

"I can't persuade you to come visit now?" he asked lightly, eyes still intent.

Robin glanced toward the house, and the man standing very still and silent on the deck, watching them. Then she looked at her father. "I can't. You know that."

Daniel looked at her for along minute, then sighed and hugged her tightly. "All right, dammit. I've told Michael I'd like you two to stick close until we get our hands on Sutton. This is as good a place as any. The girls will be well protected, and a helicopter will ferry you up to Fort Myers to see them every afternoon, if you like."

"Isn't that a waste of fuel?" she asked uncertainly. "We could just as easily stay in Fort Myers—"

Her father shook his head. "I'd rather it was here."

He hesitated, then shook his head and said, "Robin, Sutton hates Michael. He's likely to come looking for him, unless we catch up to him very quickly and put him out of action. You'd be safer if you came with me."

Robin stared at him for a moment, then glanced toward the end of the pier at the boats tied there. At, in particular, Michael's boat. She looked back at her father and smiled, realizing what was going on. "What does Michael say?"

Daniel grimaced slightly. "That it's up to you. He isn't the kind of man to make the tough decisions for a woman, no matter how he feels about her."

That had been Robin's intuition about Michael, but she was glad to have it confirmed. Her own nature was far too independent to allow anyone else— even the man she loved—to make those "tough" decisions for her. "If I'd wanted safety, Dad, I would never have fallen in love with Michael. I'm staying here with him."

Daniel wasn't surprised. "That's what I thought." He hugged her again. "Watch yourself, honey."

"I will. 'Bye, Dad."

She stood there until the cutter roared off, then turned and went back to the house. Michael was still on the deck, hands in the pockets of his jeans as he watched her approach.

When she reached him, he said quietly, "You should have gone with your father, Robin."

She met his steady gaze without flinching, even managing a smile. "Should I have? Why? Because your boat tied out there is as good as a flag in case Sutton comes looking? Because the house here is a mile or so from the Maze, and far from the girls, isolated, and a dandy place for an ambush or a trap? Is that why I should have gone with Dad?"

"The odds are against his coming here," Michael said. "But there's always a chance."

"I'm staying, Michael." She braced herself. "Unless you want me to go . . . for other reasons."

After a long moment he reached out and pulled her into his arms, holding her tightly. "No, I don't want you to go," he said huskily. "I want you with me."

Robin pulled back just a little and smiled up at him, content for now with the small victory. "Good. Now, I don't know about you, but I'm starved. Let's eat."

If Michael thought clearly at all during the next few days, it was always of Robin. He couldn't seem to get enough of her. And it wasn't just their love-making, although that grew more unbelievably explosive with every touch. And each time they made love, it was if they each knew, beyond a shadow of a doubt, that there would never be another time, ever, for either of them. As if they were greedy. As if they had both learned that the only certain tomorrow was today, right now, this minute.

Still, it was more than passion Michael felt for Robin, more than simple desire. Or even complex, greedy desire. Just being with her satisfied a hunger he had never felt before. Watching her, listening to her voice, feeling the effect of her smile and her laugh. She had gotten under his skin in a way no woman ever had, and with every passing day he found it more and more difficult to guard himself from her.

But he tried, wary of feeling or inflicting pain, unwilling to hurt her or himself. He tried.

The helicopter came on schedule each afternoon to take them to Fort Myers. Robin visited the other girls but insisted Michael spend what time he could alone with Lisa. It was little enough right now, she said, and he and his sister needed each other.

He didn't protest.

At the house they spent the remainder of their days together getting to know each other in ways they hadn't been able to explore before. Likes and dislikes, habits and hobbies; they found out about each other in the ways people always had, by observing and asking questions.

The suddenness of their relationship had caught each of them unprepared, and the dangerous situation they'd been caught up in had provided a kind of intimacy that had forced them to accept each other more or less on faith; because of that there were few inhibitions between them, and a casual camaraderie that was a direct result of what they had been through together. Those feelings, recent but unusually strong, were a solid base for friendship; the passion between them, equally recent and more powerful than anything either had felt before, made them inevitable lovers.

But even though this shared experience of danger had drawn them close together, had even made it impossible for many of the usual barriers between virtual strangers to exist, it had created barriers of its own. And they were the kind of barriers that couldn't be broken through; they had to be lowered, voluntarily, by each of them.

That was the hard part.

• • •

"It's almost like paradise," Robin said, three days after they had arrived at the house, as they stood on the deck gazing out over the ocean.

Michael, who had been automatically quartering the horizon, searching for anything threatening, looked at her for a moment and then back at the view, seeing it through her eyes. "I guess it is," he agreed, gazing at the peaceful ocean dotted in the distance with small islands.

She smiled up at him, but said, "You don't see paradise very often, do you?"

He turned his back to the view, leaning on the waist-high railing as he looked at her steadily. "No. But how often is it really there?"

She understood. "Always some darkness under the surface? Some shadow hanging over it?"

"Not always. But the potential is there."

"Your life has taught you that," she agreed.

"What about your life? What have you been taught?"

Robin took the question seriously, as it was obviously meant that way. "That paradise isn't less than itself just because there's a serpent or two lurking under the bushes. We always seem to want perfection in theory, but we'd be bored silly with it in reality. And bored silly without something to fight against . . . or for."

Michael was smiling faintly. "Did Daniel teach you that?"

"I guess he did." She thought about it. "By example, I suppose. We've never talked about it. All these years of fighting the bad guys, yet Dad never got cynical about it. He never talked the way you hear some cops talk, about being garbage men, or keepers of the zoo. He always acted and talked as if the world were a great place with just a few troublesome serpents in the bushes. No problem at all. That amazing optimism seemed to give him part of his strength. And I guess it was one of the reasons why I . . ."

"Had all those misconceptions about heroes?" Michael finished for her.

Robin shook her head a little bemusedly, still coming to terms with that particular demon. "Well, those serpents scared *me* to death. It seemed so fearless just to pick up a stick and start bashing the snakes."

"That's what you did on the yacht," he reminded her.

"But I didn't think about it—" She broke off abruptly, realizing for the first time what had happened.

Michael nodded. "That's right. You didn't think about it. You just did it. You had a job to do, and you did what it took to get the job done. You didn't freeze up; you didn't let fear paralyze you. What you were most afraid of never happened, Robin. And it never will."

Since that day on the yacht, there had quite literally been no time to think about her almost lifelong fear of freezing up, of getting someone killed because she was paralyzed with fear. Robin had been preoccupied with her growing feelings for Michael, and although she'd told her father about those fears, she hadn't had a chance to re-examine them since the assault on the yacht.

She looked up at Michael, realizing something else suddenly. "That's why you never protested when I said I'd go with you and Dane. Even though I was a liability—"

"No, you weren't a liability. You had the skills, the training, and the will to get the job done. I knew that, honey. But you didn't. And it was something you had to find out for yourself."

"You took an awful chance," she whispered. "Those girls . . . Lisa. I could have frozen, I could have—"

"But you *didn't*. And I knew you wouldn't. I've spent too much of my life weighing people not to know strength and courage when I see it."

Before Robin could say anything, he was going on, his voice roughening a bit.

"I didn't want you on that boat, Robin. I didn't want you in danger. The hardest thing I've ever done was to watch you disappear down those stairs. But I had to. Knowing you were capable and skilled, knowing you wanted to—and had to—took that choice out of my hands."

"You had to fight your own . . . chivalry?" she managed unsteadily.

He looked into those heartbreaking green eyes, and had to swallow hard before he could answer. "No. No, it wasn't chivalry. I've sent women into dangerous situations before. This business teaches you to value skill and ability irrespective of sex. Professionally I had no qualms."

"And personally?" Robin was almost holding her breath, knowing that this was it. She hadn't dared push, hadn't dared question, but if Michael was still unwilling to lower that final barrier after these last days together, then she had lost.

"Personally . . ." He closed his eyes for a brief moment, then straightened abruptly away from the railing. His hands reached to grasp her shoulders hard, and his voice grated over the words. "The last thing

I wanted was to watch the woman I loved going into danger."

For a moment Robin couldn't move or speak. She stared up into gray eyes that burned in a way she'd never seen before— unshuttered, raw. And then she went into his arms with a sound of joy that was almost a sob.

"I bet on the long shot, honey," Michael said huskily, holding her tightly against him. "You were one bet I couldn't find a way to hedge."

"I love you," she whispered, her arms around his lean waist, feeling his heart pounding against her.

"I love you, Robin." He swept her up into his arms, carrying her through the open French doors and up the stairs to their bedroom as easily as if she weighed nothing. The admission of love had broken something in Michael, that final wall, crashing it into rubble. And though that inner destruction seemed a violent thing, what it freed in Michael was a depth of tenderness he hadn't guessed he was capable of.

He set her gently on her feet by the bed and began unbuttoning her blouse, concentrating fiercely on the task. He wanted her as wildly as he always did, yet this time some compulsion drove him to rein that primitive desire. And Robin seemed to sense that in him, seemed to understand; though always instantly responsive and quick to reach for buttons herself, this time she stood perfectly still, her wondering eyes fixed on his face.

He pushed the brightly colored blouse off her shoulders, catching his breath as the late afternoon sunlight painted her bare breasts in gold and shadows. She had gotten used to not wearing a bra, she'd told him, and the frilly things in her reclaimed luggage had remained packed. His hands found her narrow waist, and he bent slowly, trailing his lips down her throat and between her breasts. He eased his weight down on the bed and drew her a step closer, until she stood between his knees, trembling, her breath coming quickly.

He was fascinated by the play of the sun on her, by the silky texture of her flesh, by the contrast of dark nipples against creamy pale skin. His hands cupped her breasts, his senses flaring at the sensual weight. The rough pads of his thumbs brushed her tightening nipples rhythmically while his tongue stroked the shadowed valley slowly. He could feel her hands tangle in his hair, and in his hands her breasts swelled, filling with the blood of passion.

His hands slid down over her rib cage, her waist, finding the rough material of her cutoff jeans, and his mouth moved slowly over a quivering mound until he captured a hard nipple and drew it strongly inward. He could feel her shiver, hear the low, throaty moan that escaped her lips. He was hungry, filled with a want that could never be completely satisfied, and the taste of her just sharpened the craving.

He found the snap of her jeans and opened it blindly, his mouth moving slowly from one breast to the other. The shorts were pushed down over her hips and slipped to the floor, and his fingers delighted in the slippery friction of her silken panties between his flesh and hers. Then they were brushed gently down her hips, and pooled with the shorts around her ankles, until Robin automatically stepped free of them.

Michael's hands slid over her rounded buttocks,

shaped the slim hips, trailed down trembling thighs. His lips remained at her breasts, nipping gently with his teeth, soothing with his tongue, sucking the hard, aching nipples until Robin could hardly bear it. Her shaking legs refused to support her any longer, and she slumped against him with a whimper. Instantly he lifted her until she was astride him, her knees on either side of him on the bed, and the heavy material of his jeans was a rough caress against her sensitive inner thighs.

She held on to him desperately, her eyes closed as waves of heat swept over her, feeling her very consciousness dim, narrow in its focus until there was only him, only him and the incredible sensations he was rousing in her body.

Michael held her tightly against him, his arms around her, hands roaming over her, caressing wherever they touched. Every time his teasing mouth closed over her sensitized nipples, she cried out softly and jerked, until finally she was writhing against him, the sensual tension he had built inside her reaching a sweet, unbearable agony.

"Michael . . ." Her voice was a shaking, helpless plea, beyond thought.

And he responded instantly. Half rising, turning, he tumbled her back onto the bed. His mouth trailed down over her quivering belly while his hands gentled her shaking thighs and slipped under her to cup her buttocks.

His mouth was fire on her flesh, and Robin was burning, consumed, and she wanted more. She couldn't hold her body still, couldn't breathe, couldn't beg him to stop or not to stop; she couldn't do anything except feel, her nerves on fire, mindless and lost. The aching throb of need filled her whole being, and then his mouth found that core of pulsing heat, and Robin cried out wildly, her body arching. It was too much, it wasn't enough, her senses shattered, flinging her. And then she was boneless, dissolving, like sugar melted for candy.

She opened her eyes at last, focusing on him, realizing he was standing by the bed and she'd been too dazed to feel him move. He was stripping rapidly, his burning eyes fixed on her. Her thudding heart skipped a beat, and she felt the ebbing heat inside her renew itself under his passionate gaze. Before she could move, he was with her again, pulling her legs high around him and sinking his flesh deeply into hers.

Robin caught at his back, her fingers digging in, gasping at the incredible sensation that was still a briefly unfamiliar one; it was like the memory of pain that was a thought, the real sensation always unexpected and stark. He was filling her, throbbing inside her, a part of her.

Michael tangled his fingers in her hair and covered her mouth with his, kissing her deeply but with a new, searing tenderness. He was still, buried inside her, the tight heat of her sheath holding him in an unbelievable secret caress. He couldn't stop kissing her, delving into the hot, sweet darkness of her mouth again and again. Her long legs were around him, her hands stroking his back almost frantically, and the hardness of her nipples prodded him.

"Have I told you you're beautiful?" he asked in a raw, husky tone, still unmoving, heavy on her.

She struggled for breath enough to respond. "I

don't remember," she managed finally, a bit wildly, the coiled tension of her body holding her in a taut, blissful grip.

His mouth curved. "You are." He kissed her again, then again, and his body moved subtly.

Robin gasped, all her senses flaring, her arms and legs going briefly rigid around him. "Oh . . ." She lifted her head and bit his shoulder abruptly, maddened.

His chuckle was a rough sensation against her throat. "Beautiful Robin," he said, kissing her throat, moving again in that delicate way that sent a jolt through her entire body. "Beautiful, brave Robin. And mine. Mine?"

"Yours." She moaned. "Oh, *damn* you, Michael!"

"Mine," he said in a rasping tone, his eyes clinging in a primitive look of deep satisfaction. He moved again, then again, the gentle, subtle undulations of before becoming long, slow thrusts. She cried out, clinging to him frantically, her body moving with his.

"Love me," he said softly.

"I do." The tension was rushing now, storming, battering her in increasing waves of pleasure. "I love you."

Michael made a low, rough sound deep in his throat, the controls of tenderness and teasing splintering to release the inferno inside him. He wanted more of her, wanted to imprint her with the very essence of himself, suddenly terrified of losing what he had only just admitted he needed so critically. Robin. Beautiful, brave Robin, with her heartbreaking eyes and quick mind, her courage and her passion. He thought he'd die with needing her.

With loving her.

The explosion of emotion was like something rupturing inside him, marking him indelibly; in the same instant Robin cried out wildly, and the hot inner contractions of her ecstasy caught him in another tearing storm, until shock waves of pleasure tangled with the wild emotions.

And though it emerged in a hoarse whisper and with his last ounce of strength, nothing on earth could have stopped him from saying, "I love you, Robin."

When she could move again, Robin managed to raise herself on an elbow and stare down at him. "When did you get so possessive?" she asked somewhat weakly.

He opened one eye, then closed it again. "I always have been. You just didn't notice," he told her.

Robin made herself comfortable beside him again, her head pillowed on his shoulder. "I would have noticed that," she said musingly. "You weren't. Not until today."

"It just got away from me today, that's all. Does it bother you?" he asked politely.

She giggled a little, so exhausted and blissfully sleepy she could hardly think straight. "No shabby tiger. Mine isn't shabby either, in case you missed that."

He chuckled, drew her a bit closer. "I didn't. In fact, you clawed my heart up good and proper. Go to sleep, love."

Smiling, she did.

•   •   •

Michael woke slowly, his internal clock telling him he'd slept only a couple of hours. The sun was setting, throwing its dying orange light through the window. He was tempted to drift off again, but a niggling sense of wrongness prodded him until he finally eased away from Robin and sat up.

She murmured something and turned her face into the pillow, and he looked down at her, tenderness rushing through him. One day he might find the words to tell her how much she meant to him, if any words could. One day he might be able to tell her that her vivid green eyes were the only light he'd ever known in the shadows all around him; they kept the darkness at bay.

One day.

He pulled his gaze from her reluctantly, looking around the room and wondering what was wrong. Then he realized. The gun Daniel had left for his daughter after the FBI had confiscated hers lay on the dresser, where she habitually left it, but his own was missing. It took him a moment to remember, and he closed his eyes, almost groaning.

Dumb. He'd left it in the den when they had wandered out onto the deck, and what with one thing and another he'd not given it a single thought since. And the French doors standing wide open, a blatant invitation. Daniel's two men, stationed outside and under cover, were watching the house, of course, but that hardly excused his own carelessness.

Some agent he was.

He slipped from the bed, careful not to wake Robin, and bent briefly to draw the sheet up over her. She stirred and smiled in her sleep, and he fought the urge to climb back in beside her and wake her with kisses, maybe even . . .

Later. First he had to get his gun and lock up downstairs. He found his jeans and pulled them on, then went softly to the door and out onto the walkway above the den. The orange light spilling through all the glass downstairs gave the place a hellish glow, and he noted that idly as he went down the stairs.

He closed and locked the French doors first, then turned toward the kitchen. His gun was on the counter beside the other door; he'd put it there when—

Michael stopped suddenly halfway between the den and kitchen, all his thoughts tumbling, senses flaring, his muscles tensing in an instinctive reaction to danger.

His gun. It was gone.

And then a man rose abruptly from behind the breakfast bar, and there was the gun, in his hands, pointed with deadly accuracy at Michael.

"Hello, Captain."

"Hello, Sutton," Michael answered hollowly.

Nine

Edward Sutton smiled, and it wasn't a pretty sight. He was normally a handsome man in his forties, with the blond good looks that generally adorned lifeguards; the past few days obviously hadn't been kind to him. His clothes were rumpled, he was unshaven, and the gleam of revenge in his cold blue eyes had escalated to something near madness.

"You couldn't stay out of my life, could you?" he demanded, his voice harsh.

Michael was trying to think clearly. "Come off it, Sutton. You took my sister as bait to draw me out, and we both know it. Surely you didn't think I'd just sit on my hands." Sutton's back was to the walkway above; Michael deliberately let his voice rise.

Sutton nodded jerkily. "Oh, I knew you'd come after her. I knew you'd suffer because I had her. That's what I wanted. For you to suffer. The way I suffered after you meddled years ago and broke up my cartel."

"Cartel?" Michael laughed, playing for time. "Is that what you called it? That's a laugh. You and your *associates* were bleeding that country dry, violating every international law in existence. If I'd been your judge, I'd sure as hell have done more than exile your ass!"

Michael had caught a flicker of motion from the corner of his eye, but didn't dare look to see if it was Robin moving silently down the stairs. If she could get into position at the bottom, she'd have a clear shot at Sutton. He set a mental time limit, knowing she wouldn't shoot as long as that gun remained pointed squarely at his chest.

Just a few more seconds . . .

". . . I'm going to kill you," Sutton was saying in a kind of monotone. "I wanted to watch you suffer first, but now I'll just kill you. They're after me again, thanks to you, and I don't have time to waste."

"Less time than you know," Michael said.

Sutton laughed harshly. "Those two outside? I took care of them before I came in here. You ought to choose your watchdogs more carefully—"

"Not them," Michael interrupted flatly. "Do you really think I'd just sit here alone, waiting for you to take *my* bait?"

"You always work alone," Sutton declared, but his eyes were beginning to dart nervously.

"Not this time. This time I have a partner. How else do you think I managed to board your yacht and disarm your men? I have a partner, Sutton. Holding a gun on you right now."

"You're lying!" Sutton shouted.

"No, he isn't," Robin said. And she took no chances; the instant the armed man twitched toward her and his gun no longer covered Michael, she shot it out of his hand.

Michael retrieved the gun while Sutton clasped his hand to his chest, cursing. Putting a bit of distance between himself and the wounded man, Michael said calmly, "Thank God for your marksmanship; it's twice you've done that."

Robin, dressed only in one of his shirts, her arm braced against the stair railing and the gun still steadily covering Sutton, flicked him a glance and said, "Actually, I meant to warn you about that. Marksmanship was always my weak point. So we'd better not count on a third fluke."

Michael could have laughed out loud, and nearly did. Instead, grinning, he said, "If you'll keep him covered, I'll go check on the backup we were supposed to have."

Robin moved to a point halfway into the kitchen, cutting the distance between herself and Sutton. "Sure. I'm bound to hit him from here."

"You could hit him from there with a baseball bat," Michael observed, and went out to check on the backup.

Sutton didn't chance it.

Two hours later Sutton was gone, towed away by the two FBI men who were nursing sore heads and subsequently disinclined to view their prisoner with kind eyes. In fact, they were rather obviously hopeful he'd try to escape so they could shoot him, a fact that a very subdued Sutton seemed to appreciate.

"I think he'll make it to Miami," Michael said as he came back inside. "At least I believe they won't kill him."

Robin was standing before the open refrigerator door, peering within. "We'll have to get more groceries. If we're staying until the end of the week, that is."

"Hey." Michael turned her around to face him, looking down at her gravely.

She slid her arms around his waist and held him tightly for a moment, then pulled back and smiled up at him. "I'm fine. I was scared to death, though."

Repeating something she had once said to him, Michael declared, "It didn't show."

"I love you," she told him fiercely. "All I could think was that I wasn't about to let that rotten, no-good bastard take you away from me!"

He turned her face up and kissed her as fiercely as she had spoken. Huskily he asked, "Remember when I paraphrased something about two-o'clock-in-the-morning courage?"

Robin was having trouble with her breathing. "Umm. I remember. You said that's what I had."

"The rarest kind. Instantaneous courage. That's what you have, love. You're the bravest woman I've ever met in my life, and I love you."

Sometime later Robin said, "Um . . . who were you paraphrasing anyway?"

"Napoleon."

She giggled.

"Well. I could have used Thoreau, except that *he* misquoted Napoleon and called it three-o'clock-in-the-morning courage."

"What's an hour, more or less?"

"My sentiments exactly."

• • •

Three days later the *Black Angel* cruised away from the house at the beach, heading for Fort Myers. Lisa was virtually recovered; the other girls had been released and gone to their various homes. Sutton was in jail awaiting trial, whenever federal, state, and international authorities agreed on the order in which his offenses would be tried. It developed that Sutton had never transferred the *Dragon Lady* out of Dane's name, so Daniel pulled a few strings and got the yacht released to him.

Michael said he'd just lose it again in a poker game. But he was smiling when he said it, and Robin thought there was more friendship between the two men now. More trust. She was glad to see that.

As for her relationship with Michael, Robin had never been closer to anyone in her life. She had never given or received so much love. And the very fact that without hesitation Michael had trusted her twice to "get the job done" in dangerous situations, first risking his sister's life and then his own, had given her more self-confidence than she would have believed possible. The demon of fear was gone now, assigned its proper place as a natural reaction and an impetus to do what had to be done.

But there was still a last, shadowy demon at her heels, and Robin knew it was one she had to face.

As the boat neared Fort Myers, she became more and more quiet, standing in the doorway of the wheelhouse as she had in the beginning and watching him guide his boat. She felt content in his love, and secure, but she wasn't certain how he'd react when she told him—

"Stop nerving yourself up for it and just tell me," he said suddenly, with a flickering smile.

Robin was startled, but not much. "Well . . ."

"I'll tell you." He reached for her hand and carried it briefly to his lips, then said quietly, "While I pick Lisa up and head back to Miami, you're going to fly to San Francisco. And take that test at the academy."

She held his hand in both of hers. "I don't want to leave you, Michael, even for a week. But I have to. I'll be haunted by that if I don't go back and try again."

"I know, love." He drew her to him and slipped an arm around her, keeping one hand on the wheel. "I've known that all along. And I applaud."

A bit shakily she said, "If you sail off while my back's turned, I'll track you down."

He bent his head and kissed her thoroughly, then smiled, his eyes glowing. "Not a chance. I'll be at the marina waiting for you to come back to me."

"Promise?"

His arm tightened around her. "I promise. And if you're not back within a week, I'll come after you. That's a promise too. I know a good thing when I fish her out of the ocean."

Robin snuggled closer, too happy for words. She hated good-byes, but the homecoming looked wonderful.

The week Robin had anticipated to make arrangements and take that final exam at the police academy turned out to be an optimistic estimate. She hadn't anticipated that the academy officials would balk, insisting that she repeat the weeks-long course in its entirety. They refused to accept her assurances that she didn't want a badge or a certification, just a final grade on a written exam. She didn't want to join San Francisco's finest; she didn't want to be a cop.

They didn't understand.

Finally, in desperation, Robin called her father, shamelessly pulling the biggest string she had, and within hours she was taking the exam under the bewildered eye of an instructor.

Still, the delay pushed her right to the limit, and it was eight days after leaving Michael when she landed in Miami, hastily stowed most of her bags in a locker at the airport, and set out for the marina. The last thing she expected to see upon reaching the slip where the *Black Angel* was tied up was Dane.

He was dressed as she'd first seen him, all in white and formally, clean-shaven again, and bright-eyed. Half sitting on the side of the boat, he raised an eyebrow at her and said lazily, "Hello, stranger."

"What are you doing here?" she asked blankly.

"I'm about to escort Lisa to that fancy school of hers. She wanted to go on the yacht—which I haven't lost yet. We're about to leave."

"Where's Michael?"

Dane grinned, but before he could answer, Lisa's bright, laughing voice did.

"Out getting a ticket to San Francisco." She climbed up from below deck, carrying a small bag. Her dark blond hair was caught up in a ponytail, and her blue eyes were smiling. "He started getting jumpy last night, Robin, and he was impossible by this morning. By about two hours ago I think he was convinced you'd been spirited off by the seventh fleet, and he'd never find you again."

"Lisa called me," Dane picked up, "and, of course, I came to the rescue."

Robin laughed, but said, "Lisa, please don't leave on my account."

"I'm not." She grinned. "I've had him for a week now, and I'm ready to go back to school. It's a short summer term, though; I'll be back by fall."

She was obviously suffering from no ill effect after her kidnapping, and the doctor had told Michael that was understandable. She'd been drugged virtually all the time, with no chance to become frightened by what was happening to her. In the end the drugs had been a blessing.

Dane was helping her out of the boat, and when she was beside them he looked at Robin, still smiling. "Tell me, was it a magic wand or a broomstick?"

Robin laughed softly. "I'm not telling. You'll find out when your time comes."

"It'd take a thief to catch me, friend," Dane told her, utterly confident.

"Never say never," Robin said, then hugged Lisa tightly. "Have a good trip."

"I will. And thanks, Robin. Thanks for everything."

"See you," Dane offered, tucking Lisa's hand into the crook of his arm and strolling away. He didn't look like a bodyguard, Robin observed, but she pitied anyone who tried to touch Lisa while he was responsible for her.

Shaking the thought away, Robin climbed aboard the boat and went below. She changed quickly from her casual traveling clothes into a bathing suit, then went topside again and settled down on the padded bench to wait for Michael.

He came less than an hour later, and her position was such that he didn't see her until he was actually aboard. And she felt her heart leap when he saw her, because his face lit up, the frown disappearing. Without hesitating he crossed the space between them and pulled her up into his arms.

"Dear Lord, I've missed you," he said hoarsely when he paused in kissing her.

"I've missed you too," she managed breathlessly.

His eyes were burning. "In just a minute I'm going to take you to the cabin and keep you there until neither of us can walk without help."

She cleared her throat. "And then?"

"Then we're going to find a preacher."

With an effort Robin managed to make her face and voice solemn. "You don't have to marry me, darling. I'm perfectly willing to sacrifice my morals and scruples, and live in sin with you."

He kissed her. "I love you, and I'm going to marry you. Say yes!"

"Yes," she said blissfully.

Halfway to the cabin, it occurred to Robin that he wasn't going to ask if she'd passed the test. But it didn't matter. He knew.

The demons were gone for good.

Epilogue

"I've pulled my men off," Daniel Stuart told Hagen over the phone, his voice calm. "I owe those ladies, and I'll be damned if I'll keep watch over them or their husbands!"

"Daniel—"

"Sorry, Chief. Spin your webs alone."

Hagen cradled the phone slowly and stared at it.

He began to feel just a little concerned.

Just a little.

THE EDITOR'S CORNER

Bantam Books has a *very* special treat for you next month—Nora Roberts's most ambitious, most sizzling novel yet . . .

SWEET REVENGE

Heroine Adrianne, the daughter of a fabled Hollywood beauty and an equally fabled Arab playboy, leads a remarkable double life. The paparazzi and the gossip columnists know her as a modern princess, a frivolous socialite flitting from exclusive watering spot to glittering charity ball. No one knows her as The Shadow, the most extraordinary jewel thief of the decade. She hones her skills at larceny as she parties with the superrich, stealing their trinkets and baubles just for practice . . . for she has a secret plan for the ultimate heist—a spectacular plan to even a bitter score. Her secret is her own until Philip Chamberlain enters her life. Once a renowned thief himself, he's now one of Interpol's smartest, toughest cops . . . and he's falling wildly in love with Adrianne!

SWEET REVENGE will be on sale during the beginning of December when your LOVESWEPTs come into the stores. Be sure to ask your bookseller right now to reserve a copy especially for you.

Now to the delectable LOVESWEPTs you can count on to add to your holiday fun . . . and excitement.

Our first love story next month carries a wonderful round number—LOVESWEPT #300! **LONG TIME COMING**, by Sandra Brown, is as thrilling and original as any romance Sandra has ever written. Law Kincaid, the heart-stoppingly handsome astronaut hero, is in a towering rage when he comes storming up Marnie Hibbs's front walk. He thinks she has been sending him blackmail letters claiming he has a teenage son. As aghast as she is, and still wildly attracted to Law, whom she met seventeen years before when she was just a teen, Marnie tries to put him off and hold her secret close. But the golden and glorious man is determined to wrest the truth from her at any cost! A beautiful love story!

(continued)

Welcome back Peggy Webb, author of LOVESWEPT #301, **HALLIE'S DESTINY,** a marvelous love story featuring a gorgeous "gypsy" whom you met in previous books, Hallie Donovan. A rodeo queen with a heart as big as Texas, Hallie was the woman Josh Butler wanted—he knew it the second he set eyes on her! Josh was well aware of the havoc a bewitching woman like Hallie could wreak in a man's life, but he couldn't resist her. When Josh raked her with his sexy golden eyes and took her captive on a carpet of flowers, Hallie felt a miraculous joy . . . and a great fear, for Josh couldn't—wouldn't—share his life and its problems with her. He sets limits on their love that drive Hallie away . . . until neither can endure without the other. A thrilling romance!

New author Gail Douglas scores another winner with **FLIRTING WITH DANGER,** LOVESWEPT #302. Cassie Walters is a spunky and gorgeous lady who falls under the spell of Bret Parker, a self-made man who is as rich as he is sexy . . . and utterly relentless when it comes to pursuing Cassie. Bret's not quite the womanizer the press made him out to be, as Cassie quickly learns. (I think you'll relish as much as I did the scene in which Michael and Cassie see each other for the first time. Never has an author done more for baby powder and diapers than Gail does in that encounter!) Cassie is terrified of putting down roots . . . and Bret is quite a family man. He has to prove to the woman with whom he's fallen crazily in love that she is brave enough to share his life. A real charmer of a love story crackling with excitement!

In **MANHUNT,** LOVESWEPT #303, Janet Evanovich has created two delightfully adorable and lusty protagonists in a setting that is fascinating. Alexandra Scott—fed up with her yuppie life-style and yearning for a husband and family— has chucked it all and moved to the Alaskan wilderness. She hasn't chosen her new home in a casual way; she's done it using statistics—in Alaska men outnumber women four to one. And right off the bat she meets a man who's one in a million, a dizzyingly attractive avowed bachelor, Michael Casey. But Alex can't be rational about Michael; she loses her head, right along with her heart to him. And to capture him she has to be shameless in her seduction. . . . A true delight!

Get ready to be transported into the heart of a small Southern town and have your funny bone tickled while your

(continued)

heart is warmed when you read **RUMOR HAS IT,** LOVE-SWEPT #304, by Tami Hoag. The outrageous gossip that spreads about Nick Leone when he comes to town to open a restaurant has Katie Quaid as curious as every other woman in the vicinity. She's known as an ice princess, but the moment she and Nick get together she's melting for him. You may shed a tear for Katie—she's had unbearable tragedy in her young life—and you'll certainly gasp with her when Nick presents her with a shocking surprise. A wonderfully fresh and emotionally moving love story!

That marvelous Nick Capoletti you met in Joan Elliott Pickart's last two romances gets his own true love in **SERENITY COVE,** LOVESWEPT #305. When Pippa Pauling discovered Nick Capoletti asleep on the floor of the cabin he'd rented in her cozy mountain lake resort, she felt light-headed with longing and tempted beyond resistance. From the second they first touched, Nick knew Pippa was hearth and home and everything he wanted in life. But Pippa feared that the magic they wove was fleeting. No one could fall in love so fast and make it real for a lifetime. But leave it to Capoletti! In a thrilling climax that takes Pippa and Nick back to Miracles Casino in Las Vegas and the gang there, Pippa learns she can indeed find forever in Nick's arms. A scorching and touching romance from our own Joan Elliott Pickart!

Also in Bantam's general list next month is a marvelous mainstream book that features love, murder, and shocking secrets—**MIDNIGHT SINS,** by new author Ellin Hall. This is a fast-paced and thrilling book with an unforgettable heroine. Don't miss it.

Have a wonderful holiday season.

Carolyn Nichols

Carolyn Nichols
Editor
LOVESWEPT
Bantam Books
666 Fifth Avenue
New York, NY 10103